# MY FATHER'S

# WORLD

## DADDIES AND DAUGHTERS

J.JABIR POPE

AUTHOR

Master Builder Publications © 2014

ALL RIGHTS RESERVED.

# DEDICATION

*I wish to dedicate this book to my parents, who remain the first heroes of my life.*

*My own Poo, Ebony, Pam and yes, even Leitha. All of whom had an important role in the inspiration of the subject matter,*

*Professor/Author Peaco Todd, who after knowing me for only three days, said to me, "You should write".*

## *VERY SPECIAL THANKS TO*

*AB (Shorty Mac) Floyd Hamilton, Mr. William D. Mongelli, Mr. Robert Pacheco, Mr. David Magraw, and Mr. Wendell Greenman, for their invaluable technical support,*

*And Dr. (as we affectionately refer to her) Ma Brown who is the project's last editor..............................*

*And my circle of Soldiers. You all know who you are.*

## *I WILL BE FOREVER GRATEFUL TO YOU ALL.*

### *The Author: J. Jabir Pope*

## FOREWORD

There is a belief in America and perhaps the world, that Man-made laws are superior to Natural Laws. The wise, however, understand that this is not so. Natural Laws stand silent until they are offended. Whereupon, there arises a conflict. From this clash emerges the Truth: that man is a product of Natural Laws and not the author of. This is a story of such a conflict...A story of Fathers who are prisoners and the clash between the Laws that govern each.

# Table of Contents

## Poo's Monologue...

At five years of age, I have my whole life ahead of me. The world is filled with knowledge and experiences that will shape me. Some of them will make me laugh, some of them will make me cry, and some of them will make me strong.

This Friday began like a hundred others, but what made this one special was that it would begin a chain of events that would put me in touch with the one person I would always long to meet, my father. You see, by the time I had arrived in this world, he had gone to another.

# CHAPTER ONE

Innocence and laughter is the anthem for these two female children, five and seven, who were playing video games on the carpet of the living room floor. The seven year old is Ebony, (we call her "Bones"). The five years old is "Miracle," (we call her "Poo"). Mother, whose name is Leitha, enters, seemingly hurried, preparing for her last day of work for the week, (T.G.I.F.), even if she has to work the night shift. "Hurry up and get ready," she says to Bones. "Your father will be here any minute to get you for the weekend."

Bones obeys. Shortly thereafter, there was a knock at the door. "Come on girl. Your father's here!"

Bones appears in the living room warmly dressed, with tote bag hung over her shoulder saying, "I'm ready." She hugs Poo and promises to bring her something back, kisses Mom good bye and turns to greet her father at the door.

"Hi, Daddy"

"Hey, Precious," greeting her with a hug. They began to disappear through the door, with Bones throwing a last wave to Poo.

"See ya, Sis." Her thin frame carried a warm and tender spirit, making her mature a little beyond her years. She had a great sense, even at seven, of how to be a big sister and practiced it well.

Her father was a man who loved her very much, worked hard to show it, and saw to her needs. This bond was not lost on her sister Poo, who followed her mother around the house as she prepared for work asking, "Where's my father, Mommy? How come he never comes and picks me up for the weekend?" Her little legs, barely large enough or strong enough, to support her little butter ball body, having to take two steps to her mother's one, to keep up.

"I will explain it to you when you're old enough to understand," her mother says to her in haste as she adds, "Now get ready so I can drop you off at your Auntie Sheila's!"

Not quite satisfied with that answer, Poo responds, "I think I'm old enough now. When do you think I'll be old enough?"

With a pause, a smile and a pat on the head, "Soon," is the answer that comes from her mother. "Now get ready before you make me late." Poo obeys, satisfied that she is closer to knowing than she was the last time Ebony's father came to get her, and excited, that she could tell her that on her return home. Mom reaches the closet that holds her coat, with the question of her youngest fresh in her mind, causing her to gaze up at the hat box on the top shelf that held five years of letters, cards, and pictures of Poo's father, to her, and another box of bears, one for each birthday. She heard herself saying almost in a whisper: "Maybe you are old enough. You're sure old enough to ask."

Well, it was off to Auntie's, then work. It was a cool fall day, so Poo had to (as her sister did) dress rather warmly and she, too, had a tote bag that carried her video games, as well as a Walkman, coloring books, and a bit of junk food for secret snacks. Her little hand was in Mommy's, as they walked down the street and around the corner to Auntie's.

## CHAPTER TWO

Forty six miles north of the city, off the highway, in a remote and out of the way area, enclosed in a twenty foot concrete wall, lies another world: the world of prison. Four square miles of gun towers, overseeing two thousand of the rejected, deprived, and on some level, the most dangerous of society. Life here was from day to day. Here, tomorrow was really not promised to anyone, guard and prisoner alike. Violence and madness filled the air all the time, and the men searched in many ways to escape it. Some attached themselves to religious groups; some buried themselves in jail house jobs. Many form or attach themselves to cliques of some kind or another, such as gangs, support groups, sports or music, which is where we find Maestro - a nickname given to Lloyd by the band and group members he formed and led. They were fifteen in number. They were the toast of the joint, amid seven other bands of various styles. Theirs was rhythm and blues, and jazz; and every now and then, they would reach out and attach a rapper to the squad, in order to serve and maintain a following among the younger prisoners.

There was "Little" on bass (the Funk Master), "Banger" on drums (The Thumper), "Big Man" and "Strings" on rhythm and lead guitars. There were also "Fingers" and "Keys" on synthesizer and keyboards, with "Brother Africa" on congas, "Be Bop" on the bongos, "Sticks" on the timbales and "Brother Breath" on sax. "Breath" and "Keys" were classically trained in their craft, which brought some stability, expertise and professionalism to the group. All the other guys were either self-taught, learned from other members in groups, or their neighborhoods, or in prison. But together, they had a blend and a sound that would surpass many of the bands in the free world that were making millions.

The front line was five in number: "Lou" sang bass and had a voice that could shake a room. He often was embarrassed when he performed because the gay guys would flip out, when his solo came. Some would even fake like they fainted, and of course this would set the crowd off even more, but with an added twist. The guys in the band could only kid him about it to a certain point before he got defensive and began to talk of war. Since their focus was on harmony, they always recognized the line and tried not to cross it. Besides, Lou was blue black, stood about five feet, nine inches tall and had a farm boy physique – naturally strong and formed. He never had to lift weights, to look like he did. He was mild-mannered in demeanor, but you always got the sense that if you squared off with him, it would be a bad career move.

"Jr." sang baritone; he was five feet, eight inches tall, smooth and mellow. His sound was even and warm, and it sat well on top of Lou's. His personality complemented his sound; he was easygoing and easy to like. Then there was "D-Man"; he sang second tenor naturally, and doubled on the leads, when the tunes called for it. He was laid back, even a little square, but he knew his job and did it well. "Shot" did most of the lead work, a dynamic front man with a voice and stage presence that always brought a standing ovation. He made it all seem so easy, and you always felt like he was having a lot of fun doing it.

Then there was "Maestro," who sang first tenor and was the leader of the band. He also played a little bass, and a little drums, and tinkered with the keyboards; so, he has a feel for the music, as well, and a sense of what he wanted. He also did most of the choreography for the group. Some would describe him as a hard task master, because sometimes he could rip about what seemed like the smallest thing. But by the time the group got to the stage, they all knew they were at their best, in large part, because of his pushing.

The "Music Box," which is what they called the music room, was a transformed classroom off the gym, often doubling for meditation sessions and other study groups of one kind or another. So, rehearsals were confined to what they could get, falling way short of what they and other groups wanted. The auditorium was located in another part of the prison, causing them to have to move the equipment every time there was a performance to be done. The road to the auditorium was always a workout and some of the guys would duck out from time to time. But, those who didn't, all somehow felt it was worth the headache to do their thing and win the admiration of their peers.

Today's rehearsal was one of the better ones; hot, heavy, and strong in dynamics. It (as it sometimes does), just clicked and everyone was in rare form and on their jobs, causing the time to just vanish. Next thing they knew there was a "Screw" in the doorway, flicking the lights to get their attention saying: "wrap it up guys, the gym's about to close in five minutes." After a brief surprise, followed by a collective sigh, the guys began to break down their rigs. (That's music talk for instruments).

"So, what are you guys going to do later?" was the question that came from "D-Man" as he took the mic from the stand and started to pack it away.

Jr., doing the same thing, weighed in with, "yeah, anybody down for some hoops?"

"Not me," Maestro announced. "I'm going to take a shower and then I'm gonna… (before he could finish a few guys, in unison as though rehearsed, said), "We know, you're going to write your kid," followed by a few well-meaning chuckles. As they filed out the door, Lou, with his deep voice pats Maestro on the back, "Don't let'em get to ya man. It's a good thing, you writing to your kid, even if you don't be hearing back. You're hanging in there for your kid and I respect that. We all do, that's what separates the men from the boys, and the talkers from the doers."

"I heard that," added Shot on the way by.

Back at the block, Maestro found that the showers were filled with the joggers and the weight lifters who got in just ahead of him. It would be a while before he could get to the showers, so he decided to crash for a little while, after putting in his bid for the water and getting assurance from the guy he would follow, that he would give him a yell. This was the same guy who often tried to get him to miss rehearsal to attend the Vets meeting.

With the ribbing of the guys still in mind, and the parting words from Lou, he gazed at the little prison makeshift frame that contained the only two pictures he had of Poo. One was when she was just days old, and another shortly after she took her first steps. In that one, she wore a million dollar grin that always made him do the same. He kissed the tip of his pointer finger and placed it on her little grin uttering, "Someday, little Miracle, someday." The yell came, "Yo! Maestro, you're up next!" Time to gather the gear, soap, towel, shampoo, shower slippers. "Damn, forgot my brush and face cloth. . ."

## CHAPTER THREE

Meanwhile, the door opened and. Auntie, wearing her best grin, slightly shouting,

"Hey, girl!

"Hey, Poo!"

"Hey, yourself," and "Hi, Auntie," was the response that came from mother and daughter in that order. "Mom's already running late," tells Poo, "Give Mommy a big hug and kiss. Gotta run girl, see ya after my shift."

"Have a good one girlfriend," is Auntie's response. Mommy, already on the move, throws a wave over her shoulder.

"Now give Auntie a big hug," Auntie says as she sweeps Poo off of her feet, bringing her into the house. Auntie's not Mommy's blood sister, but her Junior High School friend. Since then, they have always been as close as sisters and ever since they were old enough to leave home, they had always referred to and lived as such. Auntie had no kids of her own and was single. She worked as a case worker at the Welfare office, but always talked about doing more with her life. Computers were a topic she often visited, sometimes even nursing, which could work for her. She was good with people.

"Let's get you out of that coat," Auntie announces. "After supper we can make cookies, if you want."

"Yeah," says Poo, "I wanna."

"Well, first you have to wash your hands and face, so you can eat."

"Okay," Poo says, heading for the bathroom, tossing her coat and tote bag on the sofa as she passed it.

Auntie picks them up and drops them off in the bedroom, on her way to the kitchen to check on dinner.

"How we doing in there, little one," Auntie yells to Poo from the kitchen.

"I'm coming," is the reply as she appears in the doorway. "What are we having, Auntie?"

"Home cooked McDonalds, fish and French fries. Is that okay?"

Hit with that million dollar grin of hers, Poo says, "Yeah!" and heads for the table to mount a chair, rubbing her little hands together.

After dinner and the doing of the dishes as promised, it was cookie- making time. With two batches in the oven and clean up well underway, Poo, casual and childlike, looks up at Auntie with flour still on her little apron and nose. "You and my Mommy have been friends for a long time, huh?"

"Forever," says Auntie, never really breaking stride on her way to the oven to check the cookies.

"Do you know my daddy?" Comes the question bright eyed and sincere in her innocence, causing Auntie to pause and change the subject without Poo really noticing.

"The cookies are ready, and yours came out really good. Look!"

Proud of her work, for the moment she marvels at her accomplishment and Auntie, with a blow like sigh of relief, braced herself for she knows this will probably be short lived, and the hard question, the inevitable question, that (unknown to her) both she and Mommy ducked this day, would return.

Cookies, tickles, and other games of laughter, took them well into the evening, past Poo's bedtime.

## CHAPTER FOUR

The morning found Maestro at the prison mailbox, and Auntie greeting Poo's mom at the door to pick her up.

"We got to talk girlfriend."

Tired from the 11 to 7 shift she just pulled, mommy dragged herself over to the sofa, unlocked her knees and let gravity do its work.

"Let's have it," she said with a sigh.

"Your child," she replied, adding, "We've been friends a long time and I never lied to ya, and I won't to your children. She is asking questions about her father. I survived last night, but don't know if I can if she asks again. And if she doesn't get some answers soon, something tells me she will."

"Yeah, she hit me with it yesterday when her sister's father came to pick her up."

"Girlfriend, it wasn't a casual question even though she asked it in a casual way. It seemed pretty important to her."

"I know, I know. I've been putting it off much too long, but where do I begin? He's been writing her letters, sending her cards

19

and pictures, and even bears and stuff like that all her life. How do I tell her I've been keeping this stuff from her and her from him, without her hating me?"

"That's a tough one, kiddo, but it won't go away."

"Yeah, I know...maybe just a phase she's going through. Too much to ask for, huh?"

"I think so, and so do you. Want some coffee before she wakes up?"

"Yeah, that sounds good!"

Auntie said, "Hey, do you remember Kathy from high school?"

Mommy, "Kathy?"

Sheila says, "Yeah, she got pregnant in her junior year. Her father was a preacher and her mother played the organ in church."

"Yea," said Leitha, "that girl used to go around the school shaking all the time, so scared her parents were going to kill her when they found out. Yea, I do remember her. I used to feel so sorry for her. I talked to her a couple of times. She had issues but she wasn't a bad person, just confused."

Sheila said, "I know, she thought the boys would not want anything to do with her because she was a PK (preacher's kid), because they would think she was a "goody two shoe". She thought she would change that if she put out, and then got herself knocked-up".

Leitha asked, "Whatever happened to her?"

Sheila said, "Surprisingly, when her parents found out, her mother was the one who flipped out and it was her father she was afraid of. He told her that he loved her and they would work it out. He went and found the boy, which was Isaac, you know."

Leitha, "For real?!"

Sheila, "Yeah, you didn't know that?"

Leitha, "No, I never asked and the rumors had her with the basketball team."

Sheila, "No, girl that was Wanda."

Leitha, "Oh, yeah." They both burst into laughter.

Leitha, "Wanda wandered around quite a bit." Still in a fit of laughter, they continued.

Sheila, "Yeah, she even wandered around a couple of teachers if the truth be told."

Leitha, "Did she ever graduate?"

Sheila, "Yeah, she started doing the Navy, but stopped by and did the fire department on the way cause she was hot, hot, hot. Don't ya know?"

Leitha, "Ah you ain't shit, girl."

"I know that ain't even cool."

Sheila, "Yeah, but it's funny as shit. Ah!" By now they were on the floor, holding their stomachs.

Sheila, "Yeah, she was too dumb for the people."

Leitha, "Girl, you ain't nothing."

Sheila, "I know but she was. She was everybody's friend, the operative word being 'bodies'."

Leitha, "Stop, stop." The laughter continued. "We're going to wake up Poo."

They calmed down and Auntie returns to the matter at hand. "Leitha, the point I was trying to make, before we took off on this tantrum, was at the end of it all, Kathy's fear was unfounded. Her father was very understanding. He forgave her and showed her love when she needed it the most and that made her mother come around. You got good kids and that one in there will forgive you anything. She is too young to hate. Don't wait until she is old enough. That's what you got to be scared of. That's the end of my speech. Huh, ya coffee."

# CHAPTER FIVE

The prison guard that handles the mail even began to know Maestro's writing habits to his child. As he collected the mail, he commented, "Still hanging in there, huh?"

Maestro replied, "I wouldn't have it any other way."

"I understand. I got a couple of kids myself. I only see them over the summer and sometimes holidays and school breaks. The wife got them in the divorce along with the house and part of my pay check each week."

That was more than Maestro needed to know about the man, mainly because you don't stand around and have conversations with Screws in prison. I mean, he seemed to be a decent enough human being, but Maestro never doubted for a moment that if the order came down, he would be right there cracking heads, gassing prisoners, or something more vicious in the name of doing his job.

Well, off to breakfast to get the traditional gourmet boiled eggs, one slice of toast, a thimble full of juice, (probably tomato) and the bottomless cup of coffee. This would fortify Maestro for what came next.

Off to yard detail to join some of his comrades and group members at work. It only pays a buck a day but it provided soap, toothpaste, and an occasional card or picture for Poo, not to mention the fresh air that was a necessary and welcome break from the many hours spent in the cell or Music Box (that's what the prisoners called the band room). Joining Maestro at work, and

usually the first one to greet him, was Shot, not only lead singer of the group, but also Maestro's confidant and childhood friend. They were as close as friends could get in this world, with all the baggage attached: fights, disagreements, and competitiveness. The whole lot.

They have been through a lot together in their younger years and together, they even rode the railroad to prison. They also complimented each other as well, because of their diversity in talent. There was a common agreement among their following that, if fate had dealt them a different hand or the real opportunity ever presented itself, they would probably be giants in the music industry. They, together, had a clever and creative feel for the music and brought sincerity and devotion to it, much like their devotion to fatherhood, such as it was. Maestro could sometimes pull magic from out of the air, with sounds and melodies, and if he could create them, Shot could perform them with a special style that was his own, and still manage to express the taste and glamour just so imagined by Maestro, or whoever else did the writing and arranging. It helped that they had three other voices, which gave a full and quality sound to whatever the band could lay down. They had a little following within the joint and amongst them, some of the family members,

24

who got to see them perform at the occasional family events. Mostly, they did shows for the guys, and when they were in top form, Maestro would give thought to whether or not Poo would have any of his talent, and boy, would she probably be thrilled to see her daddy perform.

Shot knew all too well the thought, the wonder and the yearning. You see, he has a few Poo's of his own. I suppose what made them so close, beyond sharing childhood memories and experiences, was their lives had unfolded parallel to one another. There were some differences. Maestro went into the military, Shot didn't like that, but overall even when they were apart for years and not in touch, they were living pretty much the same way. That was always thought to be remarkable, but they were remarkable. Shot stood the same height as Maestro, and father of three, all girls. If you were observing from afar, you would find him very complicated, introverted, to be sure in matters of personal importance, yet you sometimes felt the need to gag him with a spoon. A heart as big as all outdoors, would give a stranger the shirt off his back, and sometimes the shirt off your back. But at the end of the day, wise men would describe him as honorable while the mentally challenged would call him foolish.

The yard crew on a light day just picked up around, paper, trash, and other small debris. On a heavy day they would turn the earth, haul small trees and stuff like that. In the winter, when they had to work in the cold, the first brush they gathered they would burn to keep, warm. Every now and then, they had a hard nose screw assigned to them who would try to stop them from burning their fire. But soon he came to understand that the detail went a little easier with warm men than it did with cold ones. D-man, Lou, Pete and Will arrived at the detail joining Maestro and Shot. Pete and Will were not part of the band; but part of the work crew. Now they only waited for Keys, who was part of the work crew and band as the keyboard player, which is where he got his nickname. He was classically trained. A white dude, but good people. A brother at heart: especially, where the music was concerned. He came from a good family and all that, but had a thing for nose powder and uppers, that's what brought him to the joint. He, too, was a single father with a three year old son, whom he adored. He lives with Key's mother, who had custody of him since Key's arrest and his Mom was real good about making sure he knew who his daddy was. He got to see him whenever his Mom could make it, because they lived three hours away and his Mom didn't drive. She was up in age and often ill which preoccupied Keys a lot. Even so, he was among the lucky fathers as far as guys like Maestro and Shot were concerned. Although he sometimes took issue with that, it was probably more about his not wanting to invite envy than anything else. It was his first time in the joint and he felt safe among them, although it didn't always sit well with his peers. Keys tried hard, sometimes too hard, to get along and not make waves. He was a clean faced, twenty four year old, that looked like he was about seventeen and would have otherwise probably been easy prey for the "booty-bandits" if he were not part of their circle, and was often reminded of it by those outside the group, but dare not move against it. Guys sometimes wondered if Keys could fight at all, but it didn't matter much because he was never "by himself," no match for the jungle that was the joint.

The work day in fall was special to them. The fresh country air of the outdoors and out of the city brought the smell of nostalgia and romance, which were highlighted in their music more than usual. Most bands feared doing that kind of music in prison because they thought it was too soft for the rough necks that were in the audience. What they didn't understand was that everyone wants to be loved, even if everyone was not in love. The down time on the job site was often used to plan (at least in part) their next music session. They would sit on the trail, hill or wherever they were at the moment, and draw from their surroundings and imaginations, and speculated on what other members of the band could add to it to make it great. .

# CHAPTER SIX

Much of what made the mood of their fall music were the warm sounds of the base and the angelic sound of the synthesizer played by Fingers. He was lightning fast, but had a soft and special touch that he developed himself, by being self-taught, picking up techniques from whomever would take the time to work with him. He was as sharp as a whip and his approach to things was very analytical. Fingers was one of the few among them who was actually married and had a couple of little ones of his own. He sometimes struggled with whether or not his wife was faithful and how that would affect his relationship with his children. His wife was a nice girl; shy in her ways, very well educated and independent. She had an analytical approach to most things as well, making it very difficult for them to express themselves to each other on an emotional and sometimes human level. They sometimes called him the Mister Spark of the group, but a close examination of the man would reveal a warm and sensitive guy- not very popular attributes to have in prison, but very few could match his intellect and that could be more frightening to challenge than brute strength. The emotions and perhaps the pain, that he masked so well, found their way through his musical style. Luther, Peabo, Boyz II Men, and even Michael Jackson would no doubt have loved to have him play for them. It would only accent their depth. Fingers worked in the Prison Library which was the perfect place for him. He was already well read, but a seeker and lover of knowledge, and books were his friends. He could go toe to toe with the best in the joint on any subject, and if he did not know it, he knew how to find it. All of which made him very valuable to us when we needed to research something musically or otherwise.

# CHAPTER SEVEN

The end of the day gave way to a Lock Down for a major count followed by Mail Call, evening chow, and night activities that included visits for those who got them, and assorted games and other forms of recreation for those who did not.

This twelve-by eighteen flat of picnic tables was the recreation area for the block. Smokey corners and radios on different stations filled the air. Would be Pimps held up one wall, talking the cop and blow game, with every other word out of their mouths being "Bitch," which might explain why none of them got visits or canteen, commissary orders, besides what was given to them by those they impressed. Then there was what they called the Body count wall where the would-be killers hung out comparing war stories about the so called number of bodies they left behind. Their vocabulary was filled, with adjectives like: "Punk," "Mother Fucker," "Piece of Shit," "Weak ass Bitch," and the like. I suppose the dialogue had a kind of ironic reality to it. They had little or no education, no moral understanding and no ethical development. Nor were they in search of any of the above, which in and of itself is scary. In the midst of all this madness, came the voice of "D-Man":

"What up, y'all," as he drove up on the table where Maestro and the fellows were playing dominoes. Lou, who was partnered up with Fingers, against Maestro and Shot announces:

"We're kicking ass and taking names."

"Up two games to none," Maestro cracks. "We got them on the ropes right where we want them. We're lulling them into complacency and then we strike."

The table erupted in laughter. Lou, already half rocking in his chair brought out from his cell, laughed so hard he lost his balance and landed on his ass. Chair half twisted around him, with a domino in each hand, caused the laughter to intensify.

"Shit ain't funny man," Lou declares.

"Maybe not from where you are, but the shit broke me up," coming from Shot in the midst of tears and hysteria. The group around them was stunned by the sound of Lou crashing down. This brought the attention that comes with one expecting an attack or drama of some kind, praying it was not aimed at them and finding

31

relief in the reality of the moment. Lou picked himself up and got squared away and back to the table, as D-Man weighed in again: "Yo! Maestro! New jack's in town!" (The term for new arrivals to the prison). "One of them asked for you by name on the way by."

The immediate area got quiet. One of those E.F. Hutton moments.

Lou spoke, "Drama Man?"

"Too early to tell. Your play" (referring to the game)

Lou, with his deep voice now roaring like an angry Panther. "Fuck that, we need to post up or what?" was Lou's question, angry but sincere.

Maestro spoke again saying: "No, I face my own demons, Bro. But good looking out!"

"Well, if you need me you got that. Still your play dude." With a slam of the rock, Lou spun from the waist up saying, "Can I help you Mother Fucking people?"

The E.F. Hutton moment was over as soon as it began. Some folks even walked off not wanting to endure the wrath of Lou any further. Shot and Fingers never spoke. They just studied Maestro for signs of concern, but there were none visible. Shot knew better than any of the others that whatever it would be with Maestro would be in his own time. They gave each other space that way. They didn't push; they got from each other what the other brought and didn't question the rest. But they both knew, without ever having to say so, that whatever it be, they would be in it together, in some way, shape or form.

"One rock," Maestro declared taking the money on the way out.

## CHAPTER EIGHT

…Poo awakened to the sound of coffee sipping and girl talk between Mommy and Auntie, rolled out of bed to make her way towards the sounds of the voices, while struggling to clear her little eyes with her fingers.

"Ooops," that's not quite the kitchen door. The impact was not life threatening, but sobering. Startled, and armed with the instincts of a mother, Mom was on her feet and moving fast towards her daughter, while Auntie looked on with concern.

"You okay, baby? Come let Mommy see" (while sweeping her off her feet and into her arms). She kisses her forehead and face, before even inspecting Poo for injury, which came next, and the voice of Auntie asking: "Is she okay?"

"Yeah, she got a hard head," catching herself before saying, "Just like her father," hearing the loud echo in her mind saying: "You don't want to go there."

"Hi, Mommy," were the first words Poo uttered, still with her fingers in her eyes and two of what seemed to be a hundred braids in her head, trapped between wrist and cheek.

"You sleep okay?"

"Uh huh," was the reply given followed by: "Mommy, me and Auntie made cookies last night and mine came out good!"

"Yeah, I'm so proud of you." While flashing those pretty 32' s with the dimples that caught Poo's father's attention to begin with and now inherited by Poo herself.

"Well, Mommy needs to get a couple of hours sleep, but when I wake up we are going to do something special for the weekend, okay?"

"What?" Says Poo, with excitement in her little eyes, now wide awake.

"Anything you want," says Mommy. Mommy then says, "We can do some shopping, go to the movies, get a pizza, all that, if you want!" There goes that million dollar grin. "But first you got to let Mommy get a little rest, okay?"

"K, Mommy."

This was not the first time that Mommy tried to make her and Poo's time together special. In fact, she often did, probably unconsciously, because she felt the need to be both parents to her. But now she was conscious of the anxiety that Poo felt, and was feeling guilty of depriving her of all that her closet had contained. There was no question that her father was crazy about her and until now she never got to know that. She had never seen his picture, even though the hat box contained quite a few of them, and it did not help that she looked just like him would make the extra effort to make this weekend extra special. As Auntie looked on and observed this whole scene, body language and all she knew her sister's intentions and motivations. While she searched her mind for ideas and ways to assist, she knew that she did not envy her sister in this position. She knew that when all was said and done, Sis would have to go this one alone, and that saddened her in a way that made her feel helpless.

"Crash here, girlfriend. You're already here, so just kick back, kick your shoes off, and roll up on the couch. If you don't want to do that, take one of the beds, that way Poo don't have to be running around the house while you're trying to sleep, and you will sleep better knowing she is being looked after." Mom being cut off from a response, Auntie continued: "It's settled, go!"

Auntie was a good friend (sister) but this was about bonding in preparation for crisis. For while neither knew how it would turn out, both of them knew it was on its way. Both knew that the other knew as well, but neither knew the depth of what was to come.

Well, too tired to argue with what made sense, "Poo, give Mommy, a kiss, be a good girl and mind Auntie till I wake up, okay?"

"Okay, Mommy."

"Love You."

"Love you back. Love you more."

The irony of this exchange was that it used to be done by Mommy and Maestro. Off to sleep.

# CHAPTER NINE

The light blinked once and the guard disappeared from the block, locking the gate behind him, a sure sign of drama somewhere in the joint. Moments later, the gate opened with what looked like a small army of guards that ordered everyone to drop what they were doing and return to their cells for a lock down. This let them know whatever was going down was serious and not over. The guys began to disperse with caution. Mumbles and promises of catching each other later were heard. Some scurried around in a last minute attempt to beg for smokes or books, being hurried along by guards who were already tense and anxious. After the joint was locked down tight, the word came down that the drama was real and it had found its way to Maestro's crew. It was Keys. They had not let his Mom and kid in for a visit, for some reason they would not explain to him. This was not the first time they had targeted him for harassment. They had made it clear to him in subtle and not so subtle ways that they were not happy with him swinging with the dark crew. Speculation was that one or more of the crew were having their way with him, and the white Screws were enraged by the thought. But the truth of it was there were some white guys that wanted to turn him out but didn't dare move on him while he was part of the crew. So they planted the seed with the not so bright Screws, to get them to do their dirty work. Keys knew the deal and stuck to his guns because he really loved to play and was not interested in being anyone's jail housewife. They had pushed too hard this time though. They went after his family and that's enough to make the weakest find strength and the most timid find courage. This he protested first by requesting to see the Shift Commander (the head man in the absence of the Warden). They, proud of and deep in their arrogance, told him to buzz off and threatened that if he didn't they would teach him a lesson he would never forget. But this was about family; there would be no "Buzzing Off." They gassed him, beat him, and then locked him down. I mean they really did a job on him. This struck a very bad chord in everyone, even those who were very active in instigating the harassment, because the one thing all prisoners agreed on is that family is sacred and off limits to the dumb shit that the man puts down. There would be a joint reaction to this and the Screws knew this as sure as the prisoners did. They would keep the joint locked down until they could brainstorm their damage control, gear up and brace themselves for those who would challenge their control. The joint grew tenser as the word spread from prisoner to prisoner, block to block. You began to hear cries of rebellion.

"That's some fucked up shit those punk mother fuckers did to Keys!" Even those who didn't know him or like him weighed in.

38

Now stuff started to fly from the cells, trash, body waste, anything a guy could come up with to register his protest from his hole in the wall. Now the toilet paper came flying and anybody who had been in this situation knew that fire was not far behind. The Screws took cover with the knowledge the rest of the prisoners had. It was going to be a long one and it was going to get real ugly before it was over.

# CHAPTER TEN

The sentiments expressed between mother and Poo, the same as those once passed between Poo's father and mother, were the subject of my dreams for this sleep. Our relationship was barely a year old when Poo was conceived, but was rich in love and dynamics. He would profess to be a simple man with simple ways but that was only half of him. He was a teen of the sixties, with exposure to all that it was. The Black Panthers, Nation of Islam, and like organizations embedded in him a tremendous amount of combat skills and pride in who he was. So, he pledged allegiance to family, culture and community. He had also gone into the military (Marine Corps). While they were not able to sell him on duty to country, he did come away with Special Forces training and a quiet rage that lies just beneath his smile. Yet he loved: And he loved me and Bones, he treated her like his own, (talk about irony). This blend of rage and gentleness, made our love making "Erotic," "Exciting" and "Sensuous," causing me to seek it often. Which is, no doubt, why Poo was conceived so early in our relationship, and the thought of it aroused and made her blush, even as she slept.

His rage was not to be tested beyond that, but was, one night on the job where he worked. Two fools made the fatal mistake of calling themselves teaching him a lesson in the parking lot after his shift was over. They died at his hands. The call of his arrest came at the end of my eighth month of pregnancy, triggering my labor, bringing Poo traumatically early. It was touch and go for a while, that's why she was named Miracle.

The trial was hostile and quick, no doubt because the victims were white and his court appointed attorney was more interested in remaining a friend to the court than defending him. He always told me from the beginning that my obligation to him would end at the verdict, if it went against him, asking only that when I decided to leave, to respect him enough to make sure he was the first to know, and to honor always his ties to his daughter. I did neither, not because I didn't love him but because I did.

But shortly after the verdict, I ended up in the arms of Ebony's father, briefly, lasting only long enough to rediscover why it hadn't worked the first time. But by the time I had, Maestro also had come to know of it. Knowing he would treat it as betrayal, I could not face him again. So the visits stopped abruptly, leading me to betray the second of his request.

The anxiety of these memories caused me to awake abruptly as though from a nightmare. I even had the sweats and the rapid pulse and heartbeat. When the room stopped spinning and my eyes focused I was glad to know that Poo and Sis had not witnessed this. Relieved that I was safe, I could relax a little. The clicking of Poo's video game from the next room caught my attention, but I was not quite ready to face her. Guilt, shame, and fear convinced me to lie there a little longer, alone...

## CHAPTER ELEVEN

The block was now filled with black smoke and screws with gas masks on, trying to fight the fires in the midst of a hail of debris being hurled at them. It was on, and it would go on for several days. Each time they fed them, they were greeted with insults that included getting hit with body waste, spit, burning debris from the prior meal, milk cartons, paper cups and the like.

In the pre-dawn hours of the fourth day, they came in battalions, full riot gear, helmets, and the whole nine. They were armed with night sticks, riot guns and gas guns. They used the gas guns first. The prisoners drenched their towels in the toilet to cover their face because the water and power had been turned off. There were still small fires burning. The gas mixed with them setting three prisoners on fire. You could hear their screams all over the joint, and the Screws made no real effort to save them.

Others screamed through wet towels to open their doors, declaring, "If you won't save them, let us!" They were ignored and told to shut up! One by one, they were taken from their cells, cuffed, and laid face down on the floor, in the flood. They were searched; some were kicked, stomped and clubbed.

The cops seemed to remember who had thrown the body waste and the other foul things at them, and it was payback time. Cells were ransacked and people's personal stuff, clothes, radios, and other valuables were outright destroyed. Water hoses were brought in to put out the fire and the prisoners got hit with them as well. A blast from the fire hose is an in-the-face experience, on top of being gassed. None forget, and some don't survive.

The cells got the same treatment before they were returned to them. When the prisoners were returned, they were still cuffed and made to stay in those conditions, until the Screws went about the business of cleaning up the rest of the debris from the block, which took about five hours. Then they came, cell to cell, and made them back up to the bars to remove the cuffs from each of them.

Soaked and wet, cells flooded, eyes and faces burning from the gas, some with lumps and in need of stitches from the clubs. The Screws had taken the fight out of them for the moment. The prisoners used the break in the madness to lick their wounds.

## CHAPTER TWELVE

Having rested and sobered from the intoxicating dream, Mom was ready to face her child, and the day ahead. She sat up, planted her feet firmly on the floor, took a deep breath and was about to rise, when she heard the voice of her sis:

"You look rested!"

Thinking to herself, "Girlfriend, you don't know the half of it." She just put on her game face and said, "I could use another cup of coffee."

"Coming up, kiddo," and then the voice of Poo came, "Mommy you're awake? We going out now?"

"Pretty soon."

The arrival of the coffee was a welcome sight and gave her the energy she needed to begin her list of things to do. First stop, home to bathe her and Poo, change clothes and off to the bank to cash her paycheck. Upon her arrival home, Mom found the mailman just about to put her mail in the box: a piece of junk mail from a contest, a credit card bill, and yes, a letter for Poo from her father, which she concealed immediately out of habit. It would go in the hatbox with the rest; unread and unknown to Poo. She walked in the house and told Poo to get ready for her bath while she went to her room to visit the hatbox, and prepare as well. They would take it together. Afterwards, they got dressed and as promised, off to make a day of it. The bank was not too crowded, which made for a good beginning. Downtown was the next stop, and Poo got some new sneakers, jeans, and a new sweatshirt. The movie turned into a rented one that Poo and Mom would enjoy together at home with popcorn. But not before a stop for burgers and fries.

"Race ya, Mommy."

"Ready? Go!"

"No, Mommy, I wasn't ready, now!" Down the block with Mommy behind her.

"You tricked me, you little prankster."

Laughter and hugs took them through the doors of the fast food joint. Poo was starry eyed and glowing, and Mom felt warm inside. The day was going well.

# CHAPTER THIRTEEN

The Warden, responsive to his post as the thinker of the prison, dispatched his personal assistant to assemble a prisoner representative team, consisting of a cross section of the prison population. While it would never be said out loud, it was his attempt at a truce. He had too much to deal with, beginning with the families and the legalities that surrounded the death of three. Three were dead, and many more were injured, all because a man's family was dealt with unjustly, and he was punished for questioning it. The Warden had not even begun to assess the damage in the prison. But he knew that if he did not make an attempt, vengeance would be the response from the prisoners. He couldn't keep them locked up, because the guards would not continue to feed them in their cells. Not to mention, the potential for losses in revenue from the license plate and furniture shops which brought in their own set of problems with contracts, deadlines and those kinds of things. The Unions for the Screws would soon be screaming about what was not their jobs and how the working environment was more hazardous than usual.

For the prisoners though, it was quite another point of view, quite a different focus. Justice was due for their wounds and losses in property and personals. But they knew that they had to find another route because no one wanted to travel through the gauntlet that all but three had just survived. They would call it a search for justice, but the "Man" would twist it like they did most things and call it vengeance. Nevertheless the issue would be re-visited when the prisoners were let out of their cells. Meanwhile, inside the prison, the guards took advantage of the down time. They could be found in the staff lounge high-fiving each other about hurting certain guys, breaking their stuff, and generally getting pay back.

Others were camped out, reading dirty magazines or newspapers while still others would use the time to catch up on schoolwork related to night classes they took after work, towards degrees or vocational training of some kind. The department paid for all their schooling and all things related; transportation costs, tools, books, etc.

The mood among them was high. They were full of themselves. After all, they had just had a victory against the most dangerous that society had produced. So, it was gung-ho time and Miller time would follow. Probably, before the shift even ended. Today would be their day and they knew it. They also knew that tomorrow would be up for grabs, which could give all sorts of meaning to bottoms up.

## CHAPTER FOURTEEN

The evening found Mom and Poo swimming in a tub of popcorn and enjoying the latest "G" rated video, adorned in sweats and PJ's. They snuggled on the carpet floor with their backs against the couch, but the support for their bodies was really shoulder to shoulder. Poo, into the video, not missing a beat while she occasionally blindly reached into the tub for a handful of popcorn. Mom's mind wandered and flashed from the dream to the latest letter from Poo's father, then reflecting on all the events that brought them to this point. The ringing of the phone brought Mom back to focus. It was Sis, checking in to see how things were going. She would keep it brief, not wanting to impose on their quality time, but wanted her support for Mom and love for Poo known. Mom hung up just in time to hear the laughter of Poo's response to a funny scene in the video saying, "Mommy, you're missing it."

"Here I come," Mom returned only to pay attention for a few moments before her mind wandered off again. Should she begin to read the letters in the hatbox, just to get a sense of what his mood was? Or perhaps to see if she were mentioned and if so, how? Should she try to break it to Poo? If so, where would she begin and how would Poo take it? In the midst of her train of thought, Poo reached for the popcorn again, causing her to turn away from the video, and catching Mommy with the distant look, lost in thought.

"Something wrong, Mommy?"

"No baby, everything is fine," she responded with a smile. She then dug into the tub herself and put a single kernel of popped popcorn into Poo's mouth, just before kissing her on the forehead, and then giving her a surprise tickle. Poo erupted in laughter, while trying to distance herself from Mommy's mischievous fingers. Mommy reached and got her with a hug and promised that she was done being mischievous. But Poo cringed with delightfulness, and Mommy could not help but reflect on the moment before, when she was caught by Poo, thinking she was beyond her years. The question now was would that be a good thing? Well, for now they were having the time of their lives and that was the plan: Love, and more Love. But the night was getting older and there would be church in the morning, which meant early rising. So, bedtime was near for Poo, and more thinking and perhaps dreaming for Mommy.

Mommy decided to delay what she perceived to be a long night filled with tossing and turning, and elected instead to lay out her and Poo's clothes for the morning. She began by putting on a little music to distract herself. She kept it upbeat so as not to dwell or invite nostalgia flashbacks. She even began to notice at one point that she was humming and bouncing with the beat. This made here chuckle a bit to herself.

She thought to herself, "Might as well plan the breakfast menu while I'm at it." The coffee maker would get prepared and set to go off at 7:30 a.m. That would give her a chance to get up and shower before she had to wake Poo.

Her mother popped into her head, and she wondered what she would have to say about all of this and what would be her advice.

She would be one of the stops after church but Leitha (Mommy) had not decided if she would share her latest dilemma with her own mother. She did, however, wonder if her mother in her position would have taken a different course of action. "Would she have told me earlier? Would she have kept it from me at all? Would she have made my mistakes to begin with?" This mind-set began to depress her. Avoiding this was the whole purpose of staying up. Leitha decided to curl up with a good book and read for a while. Maybe, hopefully, this would help. "Lord, help me ........"

## CHAPTER FIFTEEN

The doors of the block swung open and three, possibly four, laundry carts rolled in, with a prisoner from the new-found committee pushing each. Two Screws posted up and the yells began: "Working for the 'Man', huh?" "Sell out!" and shouts like that, were heard. The noise was quieted, when it was learned that the carts contained clean and dry sheets, along with blankets. After spending the night in the swamps of their cells, it was a welcome sight. The prisoners also brought the word that the blocks would be released one at a time for "Hot Chow," just to see how things went. So, it was understood that they had to bide their time and play it cool because the Screws would be watching, and on standby, for the first sign of rebellion. The runners also got the word to the Jail house Lawyers and the Politicians, who were already at work putting letters together seeking support from outside organizations. They had also begun to put together and make a list of the facts behind what really went down and how, knowing that the Screws' version would be blame-shifting and white-washing. One runner got the word to Maestro that Keys was in the infirmary, but doing well. In fact, because of the drama that put him in there, he was spared the rest of the drama and madness that the rest of them had endured. But he would be a Plaintiff in the upcoming lawsuit and the Jail house Lawyers would see to it that there would be at least two: one for the negligent death of the block's three, and a class action, for the brutality visited upon them. As the word got passed to the crew, in lieu of these pending Civil Actions, many found hope and comfort in the possibility of getting paid. But for some, still it would not be enough. More was due: someone would have to feel the pain they did. Someone would have to know the sorrow of the families of the block's three. Someone would have to suffer the indignity of Keys and his family. No, the debt would not be paid with just money. Some blood had to be spilled; some Screw's blood. That's the only thing for some that would make it right.

The word was given to the runners to request the Auditorium for a Memorial gathering for the fallen Three, and the request was clear and unyielding, that it was for the prisoners only. "The Man" was not allowed. It was suggested to the Warden that it would go a long way in calming the dust and seen as a good faith gesture. The Warden was cornered into allowing it because to deny it would undermine the whole purpose of the committee and its stated agenda: To build a bridge towards the healing. Yet, all that he feared and suspected would come to pass from the seeds that would be planted at the gathering.

The Prisoners Committee would put together a team to set up the Auditorium for the event. This team would also make sure that the men had in place all that they needed for the event to follow. The Prison team was purposely composed of the men who enjoyed great respect among the prisoners, even though some of them would decline the post. Maestro was among those to decline. The event would take place in the evening, after last chow. The set up team consisted of a representative from every block, so that it would be easier to pass the word around. The auditorium was designed like the Apollo Theater, complete with a balcony. It would hold all two thousand of its prisoners. With the exception of those in the "Hole", those in the Hospital, and New Man's block, everyone would show up. The staff was tense, and planned to search everyone going in, and everyone going out.

The men ate the last meal in silence but the atmosphere was electric and airy. The Under Commanders pleaded with the Warden to call this event off because their gut instincts had alerted them to the unfolding dramas.

The Warden knew he was between a rock and a hard place. But he concluded that what he thought to be the lesser of the two evils was to play the hand dealt. To pull the plug now would not only ensure rebellion, but loss of control in matters of trust and confidence.

The blocks would be released one by one, and the guards were out in force. The ones that were known to do the clubbing, the stomping and the gassing tried to look tough and intimidating. But you could smell the fear on them as you went past. This served only to boost the confidence of those prisoners who were otherwise terrified at the prospect of engaging them.

A proud moment from the prisoners was at hand. Everyone was disciplined. No one broke or showed signs that would deceive the mission. Out of two thousand prisoners, one thousand eight hundred and eighty nine were present. The service would go on as planned, with a prisoner Preacher, while everyone was quietly informed of the plan.

It was the quiet before the storm, and everyone, guards and prisoners alike, knew that lightning was about to strike, for the second time this week. The die was cast, and the air was filled with all the drama and anticipation of a heavyweight championship bout.

## CHAPTER SIXTEEN

As fate would have it, the sermon was about family and the importance of keeping it together. Leitha felt like there was a conspiracy against her, and the Lord had joined in. She glanced down at Poo, who was already looking up at her. Her little pink dress with the burgundy bow, white socks and pink shoes, a white ribbon woven in her braids, her little legs stuck almost straight out in the chair. The look on her face told Mommy that the sermon had returned her to the unanswered questions about her father. There was now a knot in Mommy's stomach which accompanied the very real feeling that she was not going to be able to duck this subject again. After the service, Mommy took Poo to visit Grandma in an attempt to avoid going straight home.

Grandma, not seeing Poo as often as she would like, was all too eager to kill a few hours showering her with Grandmotherly love that came in the form of food, hugs, kisses and pictures of Mommy when she was little. Mommy never brought the subject to Grandma, sure that she would only be advised to face the subject she had avoided so long. She was not crazy about Poo's father, but supported his rights as such. Seeing her Mother, Grandma and Grandpa when they were younger in photographs, on the heels of the family sermon, set the stage that so much effort had gone into avoiding. Mom could hear Poo in the next room with Grandma, asking her:

"Do you have any pictures of my daddy? Don't I have another Grandma and Grandpa?"

"I don't have any pictures of your daddy," Grandma said. "And yes, you have another Grandma and Grandpa."

"Do you know my other Grandma and Grandpa?"

"I have met them."

"What are their names?"

"Grandma and Grandpa, just like ours," Grandma says with a raised eyebrow accompanied with a smile. Mommy didn't know if she should continue to let Grandma do her dirty work or if she should pull the plug before she got too involved. The fact that it was getting late in the afternoon and Bones' father would be returning her home soon decided it for her. She entered the room and announced, "Give Grandma a big hug so we can get ready to go. Your sister will be home soon and we have to be there to let her in." Grandma invited Poo to wrap some food for them to take home with them, which included some of her favorite sweet potato pie, which Poo was all for. Grandma gave Mommy a look that said handle your business with your child, no words were necessary. Smothered in the hug of her grandmother she heard her say to Mommy, "Don't let it be so long before I see both my granddaughters again, okay?"

"Okay Ma, you ready Poo?"

"Yeah, Mommy. Bye Grandma. Love you."

"Grandma loves you back, sweetie. You're so precious and so big I hope I see you again before you're grown up." This was the last shot that Grandma threw in for her daughter's benefit.
Poo found it amusing.

"Oh, Grandma, we'll be back. Right, Mommy?"

"Yeah, Grandma's just playing."

"You got everything?"

"Yeah, thanks Ma. Love you."

"I know, love ya child." Grandma whispered.

"I understand Ma, really I do."

Out the door and headed home it was time to summon the courage to be brave and honest. Grandma was right, it's part of the love owed to our children.

## CHAPTER SEVENTEEN

Three long stem candles still burned at the end of the service. Each was held by an Usher. The men from the balcony began to descend, sixty in number, twenty to each set of double doors that would open out to the corridor. The auditorium sat in the middle of the prison, so the men would have to go both left and right to reach their respective blocks. A leer through one of the six by twelve windows on the doors informed the men that the guards were on full alert, and in full riot gear. This was not the way they were dressed when the prisoners had arrived. The guards flanked the doors and lined the walls of the corridor, either in anticipation of what was to come or in an attempt to intimidate and/or discourage whatever was planned.

But it was too late to turn back now. The signal was given that they were ready to leave. The doors all opened at once, and the first sixty men spilled out into the corridors at a quick pace, throwing off the rhythm of the guards, who broke ranks in an attempt to round them up for a search. The sixty resisted, bringing the attention of all the other guards on them. In their distractions, the rest of the guys rolled out led by the candle holders, who each found a distracted guard and lit him on fire. Within seconds, there were three guards fully engulfed in flames, running, screaming, waiving their hands in the air or rolling on the floor in an attempt to put the fire out. One was thrown to the floor by fellow guards for the same purpose. All the guys began to cut loose by then, retrieving the clubs from the fallen Screws and overpowering the rest. Now they were embroiled in a full scale riot for real, and the adrenaline must have kicked in, because the guys were out of control. Vengeance was now the order of the day, and this prison was well on its way to catching a bad one. Maestro, Shot, Lou, and every other member of the band, paid a special visit to those who had gassed and beat Keys down. They were very sorry they did that and said so hundreds of times in between airy screams of pleas on behalf of their families and alleged bad hearts. All over, the prison guards were stomped, gassed, beaten, sexually assaulted, and tortured. The men had quickly come to understand that they had put themselves in an unforgiveable situation and decided to make the most out of this day. Now, the word came down that the joint was surrounded by State Police, National Guard, and had gotten the attention of the Governor, the

Press and perhaps the President. Unity had to now be the drill. They turned to Maestro to lead them because of his military experience. He would not let them down. He understood that they would rise or fall together.

He first ordered all of the potential entrances to the prison to be guarded in squads of twenty five men. He next ordered the release of all the new men that were still locked in their blocks, and the release of those in the hole. The guards would be split in three groups: the dead in the auditorium for irony sake, those that were in need of serious medical treatment would be taken to the new man's block, and those just beaten, wounded, sexually assaulted, and such, would be put in the hole. All of which would have twenty five men guarding them with the exception of the dead.

The next command was to raid the storehouse, the kitchen, and canteen, and prepare to feed everyone in the joint including the Screws. In the midst of giving instructions to raid the storehouse, etc. a young freckled face kid came barreling around the corner with two amigos hot on his trial. He ran past Maestro and hid behind Lou pleading to Maestro "Don't let them get me. I can help you. I swear, they are trying to do things to me."

Lou shrugged the kid off his shoulder and Maestro sighed and said, "What's up with this shit?" The kid screamed, "I work in the Warden's office and I know where all the dirt is." Maestro said, "Like what?" The kid began, "Invoices, kickbacks, records, the whole ball of wax. Just please don't let them get me." Maestro looked at the kid and said, "You better be right." The kid began to plead, "I swear I'm telling the truth." Maestro turned to the amigos and said, "He's going to help us out. So you boys are going to have to get your rocks off elsewhere. But when the troops come over the wall, do you really want to be caught with your ass out and nuts swinging in the wind? Come on guys, use ya head."

Next, the shops and the armory were raided for all the weapons. Maestro summoned all with culinary experience and had them on cooking detail. He summoned those with medical experience of any kind, and charged them with keeping alive all the Screws that were injured. He summoned all those with military experience and had them put teams together for reconnaissance and other military type maneuvers. Others were on mule status moving lockers, desks, and anything else for barricades. A team was dispatched to man the controls of the joint doors, cameras, etc. Any footage depicting the prisoners hurting Screws was instantly destroyed. Yet another team was dispatched to the records department to get the 411 on Screws and prisoners alike. Anything undesirable in a prisoner's record was destroyed. The Command Center would be the gym, where three boardroom-like tables formed a horseshoe at mid court that supported phones, files, weapons, the base communicating system for the walkie-talkies. Half eaten sandwiches and half-drunk cups of coffee also sat on them. The bleachers were filled with anxious prisoners, eager for instructions. They loved the idea of finally getting a station of responsibility in their lives, and all understanding that this day they would play a part in their own destiny. With men eating in shifts and sleeping in shifts, while getting a crash course in military maneuvers in between, they were about ready to do business. All that was left was for the Jail house Lawyers and Politicians to put together a list of demands. The first of which would be no reprisals for the past events, and that, of course, would be the toughest to sell, but they were united. There would not be a number two until one was agreed to in writing by the Governor on National television. Short of that, they would be prepared to demonstrate that they were willing to die and take all staff with them. The guys that were let out of the hole wanted to do more harm to the Screws and wanted to do it fast. They were working themselves up into frenzy for the mission. The word got back to Maestro in the gym that they were headed to the New Man's block, where some were kept for that purpose.

Maestro, Shot, Lou, D-Man, and Banger headed off the group of them. Maestro spoke with the rest of the guys at his back, "What's up dudes?"

"It's payback time, that's what's up," said the biggest one, the one they called Big House. He was a Cop Killer and Screw hater. He was kept in the hole because the Screws feared him.

"I hope you're not going to try and stop me," Big House stated with the look that justified the Screws fear of him.

"I hope you don't make me," Maestro stated.

A look of surprise came over Big House's face as he asked,

"Do you know who I am and what I will do to you?"

"I know who you are, not responsible for what you'll try, but sure I can change your mind," Maestro said sternly.

63

"What's it to you? Why you gonna protect those Screws? You know what they deserve?"

"Yeah, I know, and you may get to give it to them, just not right now. We need them to bargain with. Tell you what. Some of the guys are hooking' up some home brew down in the kitchen, why don't you and your crew go down and enjoy yourselves. There're probably a few joints floating around as well. When we don't need them anymore, you'll be the first to know!"

Big House glanced over his shoulders with an eyebrow raised, and gauged the reaction of his followers, most of whom displayed their lust for some "Get High". One even stated, "We can always get back to this, man." Big House faced Maestro again and said, "You got that, man! You also got a lot of stones for a guy your size. What's your name?"

"Maestro"

"Would you really go against me?" said Big House.

"If you push me," answered Maestro.

"How do you hope to win?" asked Big House.

"It's like my music; it's all in the rhythm!" Maestro responded.

Big House chuckled, then turned to leave saying, "That's funny. You're alright!"

The guys with Maestro took note that he never blinked. None of them had ever seen him do battle, but had heard the story of his crime and training. What they just witnessed told them only of his courage. They would have to wait to witness his ability.

## CHAPTER EIGHTEEN

Mommy and Poo turned the corner just in time as Bones' father was pulling up with her in the car. You could see them exchanging hugs and kisses, just before she emerged from the car and Poo bolted to meet her. Ebony's father just threw a wave before pulling away from the curb, blowing the horn to get Ebony's attention one last time to blow a kiss and wave, which she returned. Armed with her tote bag and two others, she relieved herself of some of the load by saddling Poo with the tote bag, which she gladly took on like she was a little Santa Claus. By now, Mommy was squawking: "Don't mess up your clothes girl!"

"Hi, Mommy," Ebony interrupted.

"Hi, baby."

Kisses were exchanged and the two children went up the stairs, with little sister saying, "Yeah, Yeah." Mommy was trailing behind just shaking her head knowing that they had not, and would not be paying attention to her, for most of the next fifteen minutes. Once inside, they headed right for their room, with Mommy yelling after Poo, "Change your clothes, get out of your church stuff."

"Okay, Mommy," was heard just before the door closed and the giggles began. Mommy started to get settled and begin dinner. Poo and Bones would have sister time.

"Whatcha bring me?"

Bones, (out of one of the bags), pulled a T shirt, with one of Poo's favorite T.V. characters on it. Of course, Ebony was greeted with Poo's million dollar smile, followed by a hug and a "Thank you!"

"Wanna see what else my daddy got me?"

"Yeah.

The bags were opened and the inventory began, followed by Poo's help putting everything into the drawers and closets, while Ebony told Poo about her own weekend. Poo climbed up on her twin bed, grabbed and hugged one of her Teddy bears, and as casually as she had with Auntie, asked Bones:

"Do you know my daddy?"

Bones sat on her bed, grabbed a bear of her own and gazed off for a moment and then said: "Kinda yeah." Now she had Poo's undivided attention.

"I remember just before you were born, a man used to live with us. He gave me piggy back rides and (while still talking she got up and went over to Poo) he would tickle me like this." She stuck her first two fingers between Poo's collarbone and neck and Poo cringed in laughter and pulled away. Bones continued, "He used to work, I guess, and bring me stuff." Bones eyes glazed over for a moment, and then suddenly (as if she had just had a great idea) she leaped up off the bed and went to the bottom drawer of her dresser, and began digging through it and all the stuff that was there and came out with a hand puppet. Returning to Poo, Bones said, "He brought me this. It used to be my favorite," as she passed it to Poo. Poo examined it very carefully; treating it like it was priceless. Bones, mutually in tune to being a big sister, said:

"It's yours now."

Poo's face lit up, "No stuff?"

"No stuff," her sister replied.

With a hug of gratitude, Poo said, "You're the best sister. Tell me some more."

"I only remember that Mommy was on the phone one night, crying and hugging me. Then he never came back no more."

Poo then added: "Mommy said that she was going to tell me when I'm older and that would be soon, but I wanna know. She was crying?"

"Yeah."

"You think he's dead?" Poo asked with a sad face.

Bones hugged her and said: "I kinda don't think so but I don't know."

An hour and a half had passed and dinner was ready when Mommy realized that it had been very quiet in their room. She opened the girls' bedroom door and just found them hugging with bewildered looks on their faces. Mom announced that dinner was ready and to wash up and get ready, and "Poo, change your clothes like I told you'"

"Okay, Mommy."

As she got up off the bed, Mommy took notice of the hand puppet in her hand and instantly remembered that it was a gift to Bones from Poo's father, which told her the reason for the hugging and quietness. Before she could find the words to address what she had just witnessed, Poo asked, "Is my father dead?" Their eyes locked and Bones just looked on with the same intensity.

"No, baby. Why would you think such a thing?"

Poo, with puppet in hand, just shrugged her shoulders. Mommy looked at Bones, knowing that's where the hand puppet came from, and jumped to the wrong conclusion.

"What did you say to her?" Their mother said in a very angry voice, startling both children.

"I told her I didn't know."

"Poo, change your clothes, like I told you. And both of you wash up, and get in here and eat before the food gets cold. Now!" And she vanished from the doorway.

The kids looked at each other without a word, and went about the business of following their mother's instructions. Poo still had a hundred questions, but even at five, she knew in the mood her mother left the room, that they would not be answered now. She was happy to hear he was not dead, and the gift, the evidence of his existence, would not leave. It would stay with her forever.

# CHAPTER NINETEEN

Joined by Shot, Banger, Lou, and D-Man, Maestro went down to the infirmary to stop in on Keys and found him in good spirits despite his cracked ribs, collar bone, and swollen eye, which was starting to heal. He had already gotten the word about the visit the fellows paid to his attackers.

"That was a decent thing you guys did for me, I appreciate it.

"Comes with the family membership, man. Don't sweat it."

"So, the joint is wrecked, huh?"

"Yeah, along with the Screws." There was a slight chuckle when Fingers came bursting into the room out of breath.

"Yo! Maestro. They're trying to crash in through the yard doors! So far the barricades are holding and the men are there ready to battle."

Maestro, without a word, was on the move with the crew behind him. Fingers, the last one out of the room, turned and said, "What's up Keys! Get better."

They hit the corridor and Maestro instructed D-Man and Banger to head for the hole and the New Man block, and to make sure the crew stayed in place. The yard door was only eighteen feet away from the gym where the main forces were gathered. When Maestro reached the yard he found that the guys had bombed the National Guard from an upper window which turned them around. He immediately doubled the forces in the hole and the New Man block, where the Screws were held, and reinforced the barricades and patrols around the entry spots. He knew it was about to get very ugly. He summoned all squad leaders, gave them final instructions, complete with a contingency plan, and instructed them to double check their equipment, weapons, food, flashlights, candles, radios and jail house codes that they would use to communicate, knowing that they would be monitored. There were four major teams composed of about four hundred fifty men each. They were all broken down into squads of two hundred plus, and had been briefed on the seriousness of their situation.

All understood, with the exception of Big House and his crew, who decided that they were not taking orders from anyone.

Half tanked, carrying a jug of home brew, followed by his crew, Big House went after the Screws in the hole this time. The word got to Maestro who was clearly pissed off now. He took off, followed by Shot, Lou, Fingers, and twenty others, shouting to Chuck who was on post to man the gym. Upon arrival to the hole, there was a standoff between Big House and his crew, which had grown to about sixty now and the fifty that were there to hold the post.

Big House had a meat cleaver in one hand and a jug of home brew in the other. Maestro drove up right in front of him. Big House stood chest and shoulders above Maestro, who immediately told him:

"Man, I don't have time for this shit! The Bulls are outside mounting an attack, and we have to contend with our own, too?"

"That's bullshit!" Big House screamed, "Fuck that! I'm doing those Screws and no one's stopping me."

He went to raise the meat cleaver, and I don't think he remembered much after that.

Maestro snatched his right hand with his own, drove his right heel into his solar plexus, then chin, with deliberate force and blinding speed, never missing a beat and without letting his hand go. He spun and back kicked him with the left foot in his throat. When Big House fell to the floor, Maestro was holding the meat cleaver. His right hand man took a step towards him with a club in his hand; before he got to raise it, Shot snapped his knee with his right foot, and hit him with a left hook, which caused him to join Big House. The rest of the crew looked on with shock while Lou said, "Anybody else got a problem?" You could hear a pin drop. Maestro spoke to Big House's crew, "We can lock'em down or you can take care of them, which is it going to be?"

"We got'em, man."

"If you don't we will," Lou stated.

Now we heard a voice from behind, "Yo! Maestro, they just cut the power and turned off the water." Maestro knew it was coming. Now a message came over the radio in code, for Maestro to return to the Command Center right away, and he was off. When he arrived, he learned that the State Police were on the phone. Maestro took the phone and gave the meat cleaver to Shot and simply said, "Look, we are not going to play phone tag here. There are people in here that are hurt badly, Staff and Prisoners alike, and there are several already dead. If you're not in a position to make serious decisions, don't waste my time."

"What's your name, there guy?" Maestro hung up.

A moment later the phone rang again. It was the same voice, Maestro said, "Don't play with me. We are fine the way we are, your people are not. If you want to play games, you're doing it all at their expense."

"Okay. Okay, I'm listening, what's it going to take?"

Maestro requested a particular News team to cover everything; one he was sure would do the right thing. He wanted the Governor to agree to the first demand in writing, and filmed by the same crew. They had to bring in dubbing equipment with them, to make copies on the spot. When that was done, he could have the dead and those with life threatening injuries.

"Don't call back until each of these is met or the Hostages will suffer further," Maestro instructed the voice on the phone. In good faith, they wanted to talk to one of the Hostages. As he put it, under the circumstances, this was not an unreasonable request.

"One will be at the phone when you call me to say that you have met the first series of demands." Then he hung up. Maestro instructed five men to go to the hole with Lou and bring back one of the Screws that was sexually assaulted. Maestro figured he would be the most convincing. Ten minutes later, the crew returned with a Screw blind folded, tied and panic struck. Maestro instructed the Screw to calm down, and assured him that the worst had passed, if his peers would play ball. He had the job of convincing them that his life depended on it. The Screw was willing to cooperate, but it was one hour and ten minutes before the phone rang again. The longest seventy minutes of this Screw's life. He doubted very much the truth of the report he was given.

Finally, the phone rang and before it was answered Maestro and his crew thought the Screw was going to wet his pants. The phone was answered and passed to Maestro who said, in his calm voice as well as definitely serious, "I hope you have the news I want?"

"Let me speak to the hostage, you agreed."

"You shall, after I get my answer."

"No, the hostage first."

Maestro passed the phone to the Screw, who all but wept like a child. Maestro heard him say, "I don't know because I'm blind folded." Maestro took the phone.

"Your move guy."

"The Governor's Assistant has authorized the deal."

74

"Not good enough. It must be the Governor, and the wounded don't have long." Then Maestro hung up again. One of the guys asked Maestro, "Do you think it was a good idea to play it so tight?" Maestro looked at him very coldly, and in his calm and serious voice said, "You want to do this?" The guy immediately said: "No, man. You got that, I was just asking." The phone rang again and the voice said, "Your News crew is here."

Maestro said, "And the Governor?"

"We're working on it."

Maestro instructed the voice on the phone to bring the News crew as far as the visiting room gate and they would be met and brought in the rest of the way.

The voice asked, "How about a hostage?"

"I'll think about it."

"What does that mean?"

"It means that if there is not a hostage with my guys when they meet the News crew, then the answer is no!" Then he hung up.

In the military, Maestro was very good with this kind of psych game and had not forgotten how to use it. He instructed his Captain (the same guy who would bug him about the Vets group) to take a crew to the New Man block and take those Screws closest to death and release them in exchange for the News team. They grabbed their hoods and went off, with the blinded Screw pleading, "What about me?" Maestro told him, "You have not yet earned your release."

"What do I have to do?"

"Convince them to convince the Governor," Maestro softly voiced, at the blindfolded Screw while standing directly beside him talking in his ear.

Twenty minutes later the guys were back with the News team and informed Maestro that they had released seven hostages, because they would not have made it much longer. Maestro simply nodded then faced the reporter with the team and asked:

"Can we count on you to tell it exactly like you find it?"

"You have our word, sir."

He told the Captain to put a team with them and let them shoot the New Man block and Auditorium. No prisoner's faces were to appear on the cameras and they were to be kept away from the hole. When they left, Maestro instructed the Jail house Lawyers, who had already been hard at work, to assemble all the "damning papers" found in the files for shooting, padded invoices, compound payrolls, over billing for supplies, theft from prisoner's accounts, kick back books, etc. He had the Jail house Politicians do the same thing as it related to reports on how prisoners were to be treated, how to target Blacks and Hispanics and keep the races divided, and how to identify the leaders. The Lawyers were to report how they used their family history, medical records and parole hearings against them, also the files of tampered classification procedures for those close to release, as well as those targeted for beatings, gassing, and even killings. There was plenty of damning information of this kind in the files.

76

The phone rang again. It was the same voice that only said, "I have nothing to report yet. Just calling to thank you for the lives of the seven officers." Then he hung up. Maestro just smiled and Shot asked "What, man?"

"Now he's trying to play me. But I'm better at it." Shot smiled too. Then there was an unknown voice that said, "Excuse me, man." Maestro turned to see a face he had never seen before.

"What can I do for you?"

"Can we speak in private?"

Maestro scanned the guy suspiciously, "You got something on your mind? Spit it out."

"You don't know me; I just got here a week ago." Then it hit Maestro, this is the New Jack that asked for him by name.

Now Maestro was on guard and he just said, "Yeah?" The guy obviously nervous and Maestro not knowing why, was ready for anything or so he thought. "We got a problem?" Maestro asked.

"No man, I have a message for you."

"A message from whom?"

"Your daughter"

"Poo!" Maestro wondered what this man has to do with his daughter. A look of confusion came over the guy's face and he said, "Who?" Now this really confused Maestro even more.

"What the hell are you talking about, man?"

The guy began to explain, "Do you know a girl named Dana Wilson?"

Maestro paused for a minute to reflect, then came out of his thought with a smile from the memory being jarred.

"Yeah, I used to, about eighteen years ago." (Remembering that she had been the girl he spent the night with before he went into the military and hadn't seen her since). The guy went on, "Well, she's my cousin, and you two have a daughter together and she wants to meet you. She heard you were in prison, but she didn't know which one. Every time I call, she makes me promise that I will try and find you and tell you about her. I'm glad I found you."

Maestro was dumbfounded. All he could say was, "What's your name?"

"Greg. I have the number if you want it."

"Yeah, I want it."

Greg wrote it down and gave it to Maestro who looked at it for a while and asked, "How is she? What does she look like?"

"She has to be, uh, she's seventeen, man, and she looks just like you."

Maestro smiled but didn't show any teeth. Then he wondered what he would say to her. Maestro asked, "How's her mother?"

"She's okay. She's married, but the dude supports her meeting you."

"What's her name?"

"Pam"

The team returned with the News crew who said, "That was an ugly sight in the auditorium and the men in the New Man block are in a really bad way."

Maestro said to Greg, "I will take care of this," as he held up the number and then said, "Thanks."

With a broadsided pat on the shoulder, the guy said, "Sure," walking off with a kind of bounce in his step that said, I did good.

Maestro said with a look, "Yeah, kid, you did," and then his attention went back to the News crew.

He asked, "Are you hungry?"

"No, but we won't be a party to any more deaths."

Maestro said, "That's in the Governor's hands now," and pointed them to where the Jail house Lawyers and Politicians had laid out their paperwork for shooting, and instructed them after they finished to dub three copies on the spot, then they would get further instructions. One of them asked, "Where are the rest of the officers, and what kind of shape are they in?"

Maestro said, "One step at a time."

"Who's he?" The reporter asked.

"A Rep. of those you just asked about. They're ready for you, over there" in a tone that said, 'Don't push.' The reporter took the hint.

As they examined the paperwork and began to shoot, you could hear the rising excitement, "This is great stuff." "Do you know this is the kind of stuff news teams would kill for?" "This stuff could turn this State upside down." The guys around started to show pride and confidence by way of their body language. One even shouted, "YEAH, YEAH, YEAH, WE GOT THEM NOW!"

Maestro spoke, "I know the importance of what is there, but the greatest value of it is in the timing, and I will decide when the time is right."

The head reporter said, "It's your show. We're just here to serve."

Maestro instructed them to complete the dubbing and send two copies to two different people he trusted. One was an old military partner, and the other was a professional friend he had met through the music they did in prison.

They fulfilled his request and then asked, "What about the third?"

Maestro replied, "That will be for the Governor when I say so. For now, you can set up to go on the air and break the story of what's going on to this point, but only on my signal."

The reporter in charge of the crew turned to the reporting crew and shouted, "You heard the man. Let's get set up."

Almost two hours had passed and the phone rang again. It was the Trooper, who had the Governor on the line. One of the seven hostages that had been released had managed to tell the story the best he knew it. In doing so, he convinced the Governor that things were very ugly, but very organized, which alarmed the Governor. Out of control prisoners, mobs, etc., he could deal with easily by the National Guard and State Police. But organized and disciplined groups present more of a difficulty, plus the Governor was under a lot of pressure from the wives, as well as the families of the guards that were still inside. The Governor stated that he would consider honoring the first demand, but only after he could speak with a member of the News team. Maestro summoned the head reporter and passed him the phone. The reporter gave an update of what they saw. The Governor told them to tell the prisoners he was coming in. Maestro told the reporter to tell the Governor that he would have to come alone. The Governor asked that he be allowed to bring his Assistant and Maestro agreed. He was on his way, and Maestro dispatched a team to meet them at the outer Visitors gate, headed by Lou. Lou was given further instructions to take them to the New Man section, Hole, and auditorium before bringing them to the gym.

This was a risk but Maestro took it, in an attempt to assure the Governor's motivation. The auditorium was the last stop which contained seven bodies, three of them were fire victims charred and burned to death. The other four were stabbed and beaten to death. The Governor was still visibly shaken when he got to the gym and Lou quietly reported that the Governor had left his lunch in the Auditorium as well. The Governor was also outraged in part because of what he saw, and in part because he was in the unholy position of having to forgive it, if the rest were to make it out alive. Maestro told the Governor that the effect of what he saw was apparent in his face.

"The hell we live in here on a day to day basis is apparent in what you just saw." Then Maestro had the Governor escorted over to view the records that were taped and dubbed. The Governor responded with shock, but not surprise, which told Maestro what he had already guessed, and even banked on. The Governor was

81

undoubtedly more concerned with the exposure of the records than he was with their existence. The cameras rolled and all the local channels were pre empted for the special report.

The headline was: "We are into the third day of a prison riot that has already taken the lives of seven officers and many more are injured and held hostage. Presently, there is a standoff between State Police, National Guard, and Prisoners. The Governor's on the scene inside the prison negotiating with the prisoners at this very moment."

The Governor was given the demands by the Jail house Lawyers that forbid any reprisals for past offenses. Then the cameras were turned on him. The Governor opened up with:

"This is a sad day for me and filled with tragedy for the families of some fallen officers. What I'm about to do is by far the most difficult thing of my career and indeed my life. While my heart and prayers and condolences go out to the families that have suffered loss, I cannot compound that by ignoring the very real danger the remaining officers are in. I, therefore, sign this document forbidding reprisals of any kind by anyone under the control of my office, including, but not limited to, the D.A.'s office. It's the only way to bring closure to this situation, restore order and help the wounded". He went on to fire the Warden on the spot, and appointed his Assistant to assume control of his duties and bring order to the prison. The prison guards that were outside of the prison, along with the State Police and National Guard, expressed shock.

"He let them get away with this. Is he crazy?"

The news teams that were out there among the crowds agreed with the expressed outrage of the former Warden. The news team switched coverage to the satellite team outside of the prison and the Governor said to Maestro:

"I am leaving my Assistant here and you will turn over control of the prison to him immediately. Is that clear?"

Maestro summoned over the Jail house Lawyers with the rest of the demands, gave them to the Assistant, took the signed agreement from the Governor, and told him:

"When I get word that the document is safe, then he will get the prison back. In the meantime, you can send in your medical personnel, only to take care of the injured..." With that, the Governor left. The news team sent the documents to the place designated by Maestro.

The inner and satellite team would switch back and forth with the coverage of developing events. The number of the injured on both sides, the condition of the prison, and now the mobbing of the Governor by the press at the press conference on the steps of the prison, were all being viewed by the public. The Governor would have hell to pay, the prisoner too. But they had put Satan in a jar for now, and the guys could not have been more grateful to Maestro, for the handling of the situation. Whatever happens, he would be their "Hero" and enjoy a place in prison history forever.

# CHAPTER TWENTY

Mommy and the kids were eating supper in silence after the angry words exchanged in the bedroom. The phone rang and Mommy got up to answer it, saying to the girls, "Finish your dinner!"

It was Auntie on the line: "Girl, you got your T.V. on?"

"No, we're eating dinner."

"Turn it on Girl. I don't think you want to miss this."

Mommy walked over to the T.V. set and hit the on button, while holding the portable phone still in her hand. Her first reaction was:

"Shit, isn't that where. . .

Auntie cut her off in mid-sentence, "Yep, that's the one. Girl they are talking about a bunch of people being dead on both sides."

Mommy's eyes were locked on the screen of the T.V., while she felt her way around behind her with her free hand, in search of a place to sit. Finding it, she asked Auntie:

"Did they say any names?"

"No, not yet."

"Lord, this child just got through asking me if her daddy was dead."

"Where did she get a question like that?"

"I don't know. She and Bones were together and Bones gave her that little puppet thing, that she used to love so much. It was a gift from him, when we were together. So, I know they were talking about him but I don't know how they got to that subject. Lord, I hope I didn't speak too soon!"

Auntie said, "Girl, you don't think this is an omen, do you? You know, like out of the mouths of babes, that kind of thing?"

"Who knows," Mommy said in frustration. She really didn't want to think of such things at the moment. She just wanted to hear the report. The kids came in and said, "We're finished." Mommy just put her hand up to "Shhhhshhh" them to be quiet. They looked at each other and then the T.V. and what they saw was of no interest to them; so, they went off to their room.

"Are the kids watching?"

"No, I just flipped out on them earlier. They just went to their room. I think I was a little too rough on them, but they took me by surprise."

"What do you mean, what happened?" Auntie asked in a concerned sympathetic way.

"I went in to get them for dinner and they were in there with that puppet thing I told you, and Poo asked me if her father was dead. I don't know I guess I just felt blindsided by Bones. I didn't think she even remembered him. She was only two when he went away and I hadn't seen that puppet thing in so long, that I didn't think she had it anymore."

"Damn, Girl, now it's on both of their minds and I remember she used to be crazy about him too. So much so her daddy used to be jealous."

"Remember that time when Reggie ran up on him and told him: You're not her father, I am and don't you forget it." He just glared at him and said, 'I'll see you out.'"

"Yeah, he scared the shit out of Reggie that day. Hell, he scared the shit out of me, and I didn't have anything to do with it."

Laughter followed and the attention went back to the television report that was now over.

"You think he's okay?"

"You sound like you still care?"

"Well, I never stopped caring about him. It's just that after he went away and that whole thing with Reggie again and him not seeing Poo for so long. It's just a mess."

"Well, you would be hard pressed to convince most folks that you still care from the way you treated him; especially, where that child is concerned. Don't get me wrong, I'm not judging you.

I'm just your friend and I love ya, but you know what I mean. You should've made peace with that a long time ago. I mean he's good people and I consider us friends too, but I've always been on your side. So our friendship suffered too." Mommy just listened in silence until that moment, and said:

"You know, to be honest with you, I never even considered that."

"I know, but I'm not mad at you. There was a lot going on back then. So whatcha' gonna do about the kids?"

"I don't know. I feel like the walls are starting to close in now. I know I have to do something."

"Anyway I can help?"

"I wish, but I'm going to have to figure this one out alone. Thanks for the offer though."

"Anytime, you know that, Girl!"

"Yeah, I know."

"Well, look at the bright side. If he's in the middle of this thing and not hurt, the Governor says that they can't do anything to them, and you know like I do, that he's not likely to let anyone hurt him."

"Hell, that's what he's in there for and if that's not enough, just ask Reggie."

They both laughed again and now Mommy was starting to feel a little better.

"Well, I guess I better go and make peace with my little ones."

"That's a good start, good luck girl. I'll talk to you later."

"Call me, bye."

Mommy went to the fridge to search for a peace maker and found just what she needed, some ice cream and Grandma's pie. She went to the bedroom and knocked this time.

"Can I come in?"

"Yeah."

"Anybody want some dessert, pie and ice cream?"

The kids looked at each other with a mixed look of joy and suspicion. The joy won out.

"Yeah, Yeah!"

"Well, come on, then."

They were off, Mommy stood in the bedroom doorway as they passed, stroking each one as they walked by. After all, they were her hearts, her world, and her babies. She set the table with everything they needed. Poo said, "Mommy, aren't you gonna have some, too?"

"Yeah, I think I will," Mommy said with a smile that put both the children at ease. As she took a bowl out for herself the phone rang again. It was Grandma.

"Girl, I've been trying to reach you for an hour, your phone been off the hook?"

"No, Ma, I was talking to Sheila."

"Did you see the report?"

"Yeah, that's what I was talking to Sheila about."

"Do you know Soldiers, the Governor, and everybody else is down there?"

"Yeah, Ma, I know."

"Well, what ya think?"

"About what?"

"God, child, don't you care?"

"Yeah, Ma, I care, I just don't know what I can do."

"Well, why don't you call somebody?"

"Who?"

"I don't know, you're the one that use to visit that place."

"Ma, I don't want to get into this right now. The kids are right here."

The kids said: "Can we say "Hi" to Grandma?"

"Hi, Grandma!"

"Hi, darling, what you doing?"

"We're getting ready to have some of your pie."

"Oh, well, don't let me stop you. Let me say hello to your sister."

"Hi, Grandma!"

"Hi, darling. How ya doing?"

"Fine"

"How was your visit with your daddy?"

"It was good."

"Let me speak to your Mommy, and give your sister a hug for me, and tell her to give you one from me, too. Grandma loves you both."

"Love you, too, Grandma. Bye. Mommy, Grandma wants you. Poo we have to give each other hugs from Grandma."

"Hi, Ma."

"Did you tell that child yet?"

"No, but I will."

"When child?"

"Soon, Ma."

"Promise me."

"I promise. I got to go now. I will talk to you later, okay?"

"Okay, kisses, bye."

Mommy hung up the phone with a long sigh that caught the kids' attention.

"What's the matter, Mommy?"

"Nothing for y'all to worry about. Let's get into this pie and ice cream, and later maybe we'll rent a video, how's does that sound?"

The kids perked up and responded with their list. Let's get, can we get. Mommy just shook her head and dug in. The pie was great.

The kids followed suit and expressed their delight with the first bite they took.

Mommy's mind began to wander again, and it took her back to the prison visit, when Maestro first laid eyes on Poo. He was the happiest man and father in the world, and she never felt more loved and proud. The reflection made her grin unconsciously, causing the kids to giggle and return her to the moment.

"What's so funny?"

"Your face Mommy," then they giggled again.

"Oh, y'all are laughing at me, huh?" Mommy said as she rose from the table moving her fingers playfully like the claws of a monster and the kids took off. Poo, going under the table, and Bones around and out the kitchen door laughing, with Mommy right on her heels.

"I'm gonna get ya."

The laughter escalated. They were in for tickles and wrestling, and the hurt feelings that were there before supper seem light years away now. All was well for the moment, Mommy thought, but how long will the moment last?

# CHAPTER TWENTY ONE

The medical team had come in to attend to the injured guards and prisoners, relieving the prisoners of that chore. The power, the water, and prisoners' phones were turned back on. The Governor's Assistant had agreed to enough of the demands to satisfy most of the population and the document had been delivered. Maestro had only two requests left, that the news crew film the return of the prison to the authorities, so they could not claim that they resisted once they were back in the prison; and that any prisoner that wished to, could call his family and let them know that he was alright. Both requests were agreed to and some of the guys who did not have family decided to call the families of those that had fallen in the riot. The count was five prisoners dead, thirty one injured. Maestro would use his call to reach his eldest daughter, he had the word passed and the calls were under way.

It was Maestro's daughter, Pam, who took the call. The first thing she did after telling the operator that yes, she would accept the call, was scream "It's him! It's him!"

"Hi, Daddy!"

"Hi, sweetheart."

"I've been trying to find you for years."

"Well, congratulate me."

Pam sounded confused and said, "For what?"

"It's a girl."

She paused and burst into laughter, screaming, "I get it, you're funny." Her laughter was infectious, and Maestro laughed also. Then Pam said, "You must have met Greg."

"Yep! That's who gave me your number."

"Tell him I love him for finding you. We were watching this stuff on television about a riot; that's not the prison you all are at, is it?"

"Yep, it is."

"It is! Oh, my God is Greg alright?"

"Yeah, he's okay."

"I want to see you. Can I see you, will they let me? I have a thousand questions."

"I could probably arrange it, but it may take a while because of all this stuff that's going on around here. If I'm able to arrange it, how will you get here?"

"I have my license and my cousin will let me use her car. Can I write you?"

"Sure."

"I'm going to write you tonight, okay?"

"Sure, it's okay. Will you send me a picture, too?"

"Yeah. Do I have any brothers or sisters?"

"Yep. You have a little sister. She's five."

"What's her name? Where does she live?"

"Where do you live?"

"On Madison Street."

"Is that right?"

"Yeah."

"She only lives about fifteen blocks from you."

"Can I go see her?"

"I would like that. I haven't been able to see her since she was in diapers."

"Let me get something to write with so I can take down the address." She left the phone off the hook, and Maestro looked over his shoulder to see two guys still waiting for the phone. He told them he'd be off in a minute. She was back on the line saying:"O.K., give me the address." Maestro did. She said, "Let me get your address, too," and he gave it to her. He asked, "How are you doing in school?"

"Straight A's."

"Well, take a bow."

She giggled. He said, "Well, sweetheart, I have to go. People are waiting to use the phone, but I will call again as soon as I can, and I will answer your letters as soon as I get them."

"You want to speak to Morn?"

"I can't this time, next time, okay?"

"Okay."

"I'm happy to know I have another daughter, and I will think about you every minute, until I meet you, and then every minute after that."

"I will too."

"That's my girl. I love you."

"I love you too."

He could hear her say under her breath, "Yeah, I got a little sister." Then she said to Maestro, "I'm going to try to see her today. I can't wait and I'll tell you all about it in my letter." Maestro said, "Pam, go slow, sweetheart, you're going to be taking everyone by surprise, Poo, her mother and her sister. Do you understand?"

"Yes, Daddy, I understand."

"It feels good to hear that."

"What?"

"Daddy"

"Oh!"

In a way, that let Maestro know she just did it naturally and unconsciously. Maestro said, "Got to let you go sweetheart, but we'll be in touch soon. Love you."

"Love you, too. Bye."

"Bye."

When the last of the guys got off the phone, Maestro summoned his team captains and instructed them to instruct everyone to put down their weapons, and return to their cells. He then had the keys to the joint turned over to the Governor's Assistant, shook the hands of the news crew and thanked them for all they had done, as well as for sticking around to make sure the transformation was made without incident. They thanked him for his confidence in them, and wished them good luck.

Maestro faced the Governor's Assistant and said, "It's your joint again, be wise." Then he returned to his cell.

His head was now spinning with thoughts of Poo and his new found daughter. How did Pam look? How much did Poo grow? How did Pam's mother look and how would she act towards him. How would Poo and her mother respond to Pam's existence and arrival? His thought pattern was interrupted with the sound of a Screw bellowing, "Everyone in your own cell, now!" The doors slammed and he yelled again to another crew of Screws, "Start your count," and as the numbers began to echo through the block, Maestro was in wonder of what would come next. He laid down not realizing how exhausted he was from the whole ordeal, and his thoughts raced back and forth from family to speculation of what was to come. Then, without even noticing it, he was overtaken by sleep.

## CHAPTER TWENTY TWO

Poo had just gotten into the bath tub when there was a knock, and her mother went to answer it. Mom opened the door to a tall slender, beautiful girl of seventeen, who she had never laid eyes on before, but for some reason looked familiar. She was stylishly dressed in a casual way. Blue jeans that looked like they were tailored, sat on top of black boots with a round toe that displayed white stitching, a blue blouse that tied at the neck, and a leather wrap around sport coat. Her hair fell over her shoulders straight and shining with a very healthy look and her petite face was without blemish. Her lips parted to reveal very well kept, bright white teeth, as she said:

"Hi, is this where Poo lives?"

A look of confusion came over Mom's face as she said, "You're a little old to be playing with Poo, aren't you?" Pam, caught off guard, giggled, and then remembering the words of her father, she said, "I'm sorry, I know this seems odd, but I just found out that she is my sister. Are you her mother?"

Mom placed her left hand over her breast as if to catch her breath, with the look of confusion now upgraded to shock, yet at the same moment it hit her why this girl looked so familiar. She not only looked like Poo's father, she looked like Poo also.

"Come in," Mom said, stuttering. The young lady spoke again.

"My father told me I would be taking everyone by surprise;" as she came through the door and began to look around, she said, "Please forgive me. I don't mean to upset you or anything, I'm just kind of anxious to meet her. I don't have any other sisters or brothers and I just found out about her today."

Mom's observation of her was that she was polite and sincere, and now Mom was seized by curiosity.

"Sit."

"Thank you. You have a nice home."

"Thank you. What's your name?"

"Pam."

"You said your father told you about Poo, and that you just found out today."

"Yes."

"So, you spoke to him today?"

"Yes, about two hours ago."

"You speak with him a lot?"

"Today was the first time."

"Oh!"

"Yeah, my cousin is in that place with him, and he gave him my number and told him that I was trying to find him, so he called. When he did, I asked if I had any sisters or brothers, and he told me about Poo."

"So you haven't met him yet?"

"No, Ma'am."

"Please don't call "Ma'am"."

Pam just kind of smiled and Mom gave her the kind of grin that said, "Be at ease, but don't go there."

Pam spoke, "Can I ask you something?"

"Yes."

"Do you have a picture of him?"

At that moment Bones walked into the living room on her way to hurry Poo, so she could take her bath. Pam's glance went from Bones to Mom, and her expression asked the question "Is this her?" Mom being able to read the expression spoke, saying, "This is Ebony, Miracle's sister."

Bones said, "Hi." And so did Pam.

Mom said, "And this is Pam."

Bones continued on to the bathroom and knocked. You could hear her saying, "I'm coming in. It's my turn." And Poo saying, "I'm coming."

Pam gave Mom that look again, and now she knew that was the voice of her sister.

Mom said, "Well, I knew it was coming sooner or later. I guess it's time, Excuse me for a moment."

"Sure."

Mom disappeared into her bedroom. In her absence; Poo came out of the bathroom with a towel wrapped around her from chin to shin. When she was on her way through the living room, she looked at Pam curiously, and said, "Hello."

"Hi, you want some help drying off?"

Poo hunched her shoulders and Pam told her to get her clothes and another towel, and she did. When she returned Pam began to dry her off, and said to her,

"My name is Pam."

"My name is Poo."

Pam just smiled and said, "I know." Pam then ran the towel through Poo's hundred braids and said, "You have a nice head of hair."

Poo now had a strand of Pam's shoulder length hair between her fingers and said, "You got nice hair, too."

Mom walked in to witness this Kodak moment, with the hat box in her hands, wondering how much Pam had told Poo, and was relieved to learn that there had been nothing said on the pending subject. Mom set the hat box, unopened, on the table in front of the couch and took over the task of drying Poo and helping her put on her P.J.'s. When she had finished, she hugged her and then said, as she held her almost arm's length, "You know Momma loves you right?"

With a curious look, Poo said, "Yes," while glancing at Pam for some sign of what this was all about.

"Mommy knows you have been asking a lot of questions lately. Well, it's time you got some answers."

Poo looked up at her mother with excitement and anticipation and said, "You mean about my Daddy?"

Mom nodded her head and said, "About your daddy!"

Poo's face was lit up now, not with a smile, but joy expressed itself clearly through her wiggly little body.

Mom asked Pam to pass her the hat box as she turned Poo away from her and then pulled her up onto her lap. When Pam passed Mom the hat box, she placed it in her and Poo's lap. Then Mom patted a spot beside her, indicating to Pam to sit closer, which she gladly did. Poo's excitement was mixed with curiosity, struggling to try and figure out what this person has to do with her daddy. Mom opened the hat box and the first thing she removed was Maestro's most recent picture to Poo. Mommy simply said, "Girls, this is your father." Poo immediately took the picture from her mother for a closer look, as Pam leaned over to do the same, causing Poo to look up at her and then her mother, asking "Is this her daddy too?"

"Yes, baby, this is your sister."

She looked at Pam who smiled at her and said, "Hi, sis. Pleased to meet ya." Poo gazed at her mother again to check to make sure this was real. Mom showed no signs that this was a joke, and then Poo asked, "Is Bones still my sister?"

Mom smiled and said, "Of course, she is. You have two sisters now." Then she looked at Pam again.

Pam then asked, "Can I have a hug?"

Poo looked up at her mother who gave her a nod. Then Poo climbed down and went to the waiting arms of her sister who hugged her, and then pulled her up on her lap. Then they began to study the picture together.

Bones came out of the bathroom and Poo looked up and hollered to her, "Bones we have a new sister. Her name is Pam!"

Bones stopped in her tracks and Mom and Pam just looked at each other with that "she doesn't understand" look.

Meanwhile, Bones studied everyone curiously. Poo continued, "Look, Bones, a picture of my daddy." She was down and heading for Bones by this time, and Mom looked over at Pam, reached into the box for another picture and passed it to Pam, saying, "Here's another."

Pam took it and began to study it as well. Then Pam asked, "Do you go to see him?"

Mom, embarrassed by the question, just said, "Not in a long time." Pam just responded, "Okay," and returned her attention to the picture, while leaving Mom to wonder if she was being judged.

Then Pam asked, "Do you think I look like him?"

Mom responded with, "As a matter of fact you do. I noticed that right off."

Pam then asked, "You think we look alike?" referring to her and Poo.

Mom said, "A little."

Now Poo was back with Bones standing by her side, and asking the question, "Is he coming to see me?" Now Mommy was stuck. She knew she had a good reason for ducking the question for so long. Questions like this were the reason.

She said, "See all these letters in the box?"

"They're all to you from your father." Poo's face was bright again as she said, "They are?" Her Mom said, "Yep." Then Poo asked, "What do they say?"

Mom, with half a chuckle, said, "They say a lot of stuff."

Poo asked, "Will you read them to me?" with that million dollar smile on her face.

Mom responded, "Yeah, but a little later, okay?"

Poo says, "Okay. So when is he coming?"

Pam cut Mom off and asked if she could speak with her in private.

"Ah huh, sure," Mom said. "We'll be right back, in here," she says as they walked into the kitchen, happy for the break but bracing herself for the unknown.

Pam said, "I didn't want to get her hopes up before talking with you, but my father says he will make arrangements for me to see him. I would love to take her with me, if it's okay with you."

Mom responded, "Well, I would have to think about it. When is this all supposed to be happening?"

Pam said, "I'm not sure yet, but it probably won't be for a couple of weeks, at least."

Mom replied, "Oh, okay then. Well, we have a little time yet."

Pam smiled and said, "Yeah, in the meantime, if it's okay, I would like to visit Poo, maybe take her out shopping, to a movie, and stuff like that. Okay?"

Mother says, "I don't see anything wrong with that, as long as she wants to go. But you understand I need to know more about you, where you live, family and those sorts of things."

Pam replies, "Oh, yes, I understand, and listen if you want me to read those letters to her, I'll be happy to."

Mom rubbed her forehead with the feeling that this is all happening too fast, and then said, "No, I think I better do that. But you're welcome to keep the picture if you like."

Pam happily said, "Thank you, I would like that."

"Would you like something to drink, some juice or some soda or something?"

"No, thank you, but I would like to spend some more time with Poo this evening, if I could. What time does she go to bed?"

"Well, it's Sunday night, and she does have to go to school in the morning."

"God, so do I," Pam said, "My family will be expecting me back soon."

Mom said, "Well, she might not get much sleep tonight anyway, with the news she just got. So, I guess it will be okay for you to stay a while longer. You can join them while I get a pencil so I can get your address and phone number.

"Okay, thank you."

Mom headed to the bedroom and Pam returned to the living room where Poo and Bones had gotten into the hat box, and they had all the pictures out and scattered on the rug. They were just looking at them, pointing and talking. Bones reached for the other box saying, "Is this some more?" When she opened the box she said, "Ooo, Poo look." There were five little bears in the box. One for each birthday, and each one is a little bigger than the year before. They all had little t-shirts on them that said loving things. The last and biggest of them said, "Hey Poo, guess who loves you? Daddy Do." Poo hit her sister with that million dollar grin and said, "This is mine?" Bones said, "Yep." Poo asked, "What they say? Tell me! What they say?" Bones said "Slow down, I'm gonna." Then Bones began to read the t-shirts to Poo. Pam joined them by sitting on the floor, and Poo said to her, "Do daddy come and see you?"

"No, but I talked to him on the phone today."

She now had both of their attention.

"You did?"

"Yep. That's when he told me about you, and asked me to come and see you, and tell you that he loves and misses you."

"He did?"

"Yep, and he said something else too."

"What?"

"He said he wants us to be close and love each other."

Poo looked down at the pictures again, then hugged Pam and said,

"You're really my big sister?"

Pam responded, "Yep, I really am."

Then Pam extended a hand for Bones to join them in a group hug. She took them up on it. Poo took the biggest, the smallest, and the middle bear and ran to her room with them. When she came back, she gave each of her sisters one of the remaining bears. They both thanked her and resumed the group hug. Mom looked on from the doorway, feeling like a great weight had been lifted from her shoulders. But now she wondered what this revelation represented. She never knew Lloyd had another child. Now the question is, who was her mother, have they been in touch over the years? Well, she would worry about that later.

Poo asked Pam, "When can I talk to my father?"

Pam said, "Well, I promised him I would write him a letter tonight after I saw you. You want to write it together?"

"Will that be okay?" Pam asked her mother.

"Sure. I'll get you everything you need."

"You mind if I use your phone to tell my Mom I'm going to be a little late?"

"No, go right ahead."

Mom headed for the bedroom and Pam went to the phone. Poo and Bones were at the pictures again, trying to figure out the background. Bones pulled a letter out of the box that had more pictures in it of Maestro with the band. The two of them marveled over them.

Mom returned with a full set of writing supplies, complete with stamps and envelopes. Pam summoned Poo's mom to the phone.

"My Mom would like to talk to you." Poo's mom took the phone and said, "Hello" to a very nice voice that introduced herself and apologized for her daughter crashing into her life as she did.

"It was a surprise I admit I was not prepared for. But it's alright. She seems very nice"

"Listen, I'm sure you have curiosities, would you like to have lunch sometime? We can talk and get to know each other better, since we have something permanently in common." They both kind of chuckled a little, and then Poo's mother said, "That sounds like a good idea. Let me give you my number, okay."

"And here's mine."

They wrapped up their call, and Mom turned to Pam and handed her the writing supplies, and said, "Your mother sounds like a very nice person."

Pam said, "Yes, she is, and so are you."

Mom kind of blushed and said, "You two better get started."

You did not have to tell Poo twice. She grabbed her sister by the hand and started tugging her towards the kitchen to the table.

Mom walked over and grabbed Bones from behind, wrapping her arms around Bones shoulder and putting her head first on top of Bones and then at the side of her face, and asking, "What do you think of all this?"

Bones looked up at her mother and said, "She's happy. She got her questions answered and she got another sister out of the deal. I guess it's okay. Did she bring those pictures and letters here?"

"No, those things have been in my closet for a long time now."

Bones seemed surprised, but questioned no further.

"Where is he anyway?"

Mom looked at her, then away and said, "Prison."

"What did he do?"

"It's a long story."

"I remember him a little. I remember he used to give me piggy back , I remember he gave me Mr. Puppet, and I remember you crying one night on the phone. Then he never came home. Did he do something to you?"

"No, nothing like that. You remember that far back?"

"Yeah."

"Well, I was crying that night because I knew he couldn't come back, okay?"

"Okay."

"Well, you got school tomorrow, so, you ready to turn in?"

"Is she staying here?"

"No, she'll be leaving as soon as they finish."

"I like her, Poo is lucky."

Mom hugged her around the shoulders again, this time kissing her on top of her head saying, "No sweetie, she just got a little luckier maybe, but she's always been lucky because she always had you, and you wanna know something else, I'm lucky too, for having you."

Bones smiled and cuddled her mother's arms, tipped her head back, and they kissed each other. Bones broke the hold and said, "I'm going in the kitchen to say goodnight." She went to the kitchen door and just said, "Goodnight."

Pam looked up and said, "Goodnight, Ebony."

Ebony went off to her room feeling good for her sister and about her mother.

Mom picked up the phone and dialed. A moment later Auntie picked up the phone, "What'cha doing girl?"

"Watching T.V."

"You will, never guess who is in my kitchen."

"Denzel Washington."

"No, girl," they both laughed.

"No, who?"

"Are you sitting down?"

"Yeah, girl. I'm watching T.V. Who already!"

"Poo's sister."

"Bones?"

"No, her big sister."

"Girl, what are you talking about? Poo don't have no big sister.

"Yeah, she does."

"Ooooh, girl, don't tell me. . .

"Yeah, girl, she showed up tonight saying her father sent her to see Poo."

"Girl, let me turn the set off. How she look?"

"Like him."

"Lord, how old is she?"

"Seventeen"

"So who does Poo think she is?"

"She knows. When the child showed up, I had to tell her. They're there now with the pictures all over the place, writing him a letter together."

"Well, I'll be fitted for a heart attack."

"Tell me about it!"

"So, how did it go? Telling her, I mean?"

"Well, it wasn't no drama or trauma if that's what you mean. But there was plenty for her to be distracted by, with a new sister and all. But I know there will be a thousand questions when this girl leaves. Poo already asked when he's coming to see her."

"She doesn't know where he is yet?"

"No."

"Does the other one know where he is?"

"Yeah. She knows. She talked to him today."

"Did he tell her about all the mess up there?"

"I don't know, girl. It never came up. You're so nosy."

"You want to know too, and you know you do."

"Right now, I just want to get through the night."

"Girl, I know that. So, tell me some more about her."

"She's nice enough, I guess. She seems to be well brought up. I spoke with her mother as well, who invited me to lunch so we can get together and get to know each other better, don't cha know."

"Uh huh." (They both giggled like two school girls.) "She's trying to size you up girlfriend."

"Don't start."

"Okay, but remember who told you so."

"Listen girl, I'm gonna let you go."

"No girl! You better not hang up this phone."

"Girl look, my head is still spinning from all this and I don't want them to hear us. So, I'll call you back after she goes and the kids are in bed."

"You promise?"

"Okay girl. Don't make me come over there now." They chuckled again and Mom said, "Girl, you're too much, I'll get back at 'cha." Then she hung up.

Mom walked into the kitchen as they were finishing up the letter, and she heard Pam ask Poo, did she have a picture of herself that she wanted to send? Poo turned to her mother,

"Mommy, do I have any pictures?"

111

"Yep, just a minute." And she disappeared into her bedroom. She returned a moment later, with a small wallet size picture of Poo.

"Here you go; this should fit in that envelope."

Poo took it, looked at it, then passed it to Pam, who put it in the envelope and said, "I'm going to mail this from home, because I want to put a picture in it too, okay?"

Poo just nodded, and then Pam leaned over and bumped her shoulder lightly against Poo's and said, "So, how do you like having another big sister?"

Poo hit her with that smile of hers that was flavored with a bit of shyness and said, "Fine."

Pam rose and said, "Wanna walk me to the door little sis?"

Poo climbed down off the chair and they joined hands and started toward the door with Pam saying, "I'll call you tomorrow, okay?"

Poo said, "Okay." Then Pam knelt down and said, "Can I have a hug?" Poo gave her a real good one, and Pam removed a bracelet from her wrist and handed it to Poo.

"Take care of that for me, okay?"

"Okay."

Pam turned to Poo's mom and said, "Thank you for having me in your home."

"It's okay; I mean you're my daughter's family."

Pam held up the picture given to her and said, "Thanks for this also. I really appreciate it."

"No problem."

Poo said, "Don't forget your Daddy bear."

Pam said, "Okay."

Pam touched Poo on the nose and said to both of them, "Say bye to Bones for me, will ya?"

"Sure. Are you going to be alright? Do you want to call a cab or something?"

"No, thank you, I'll be okay. See ya."

"Okay."

As she shut the door, Mommy looked down into the face of her youngest which was full of questions. She sighed and said, "How about you sleeping with me tonight?"

Poo said, "Okay." Mom went to look in on Bones to say goodnight, and to tell her of the sleeping plans, then she thought better of it, and said, "Why don't we all sleep together tonight and I can answer everyone's questions? How's that sound, good?"

"Yeah, good."

"Okay, then, let's go." Poo said, "Mommy you want a Daddy bear?" "No, sweetheart, those are for you, but thank you baby."

All three were off to Mommy's room for the slumber party that would answer old questions and create greater bonding.

## CHAPTER TWENTY-THREE

Five days into the lock down, while the staff was still cleaning up, and planning the future running of the jail, there was finally a mail delivery cell to cell. As fate would have it, Maestro's was delivered by the same Screw who would comment on his mailing habits and also among those in the hole whose hide was saved by Maestro, when Big-House and his crew attempted to move against them, and he knew it. He placed the letter on the bar saying, "Well guy, it looks like your diligence might of paid off."

Maestro said, "You've been reading my mail?"

"Not I, but the truth is, between you and I, not only has it been read but there is a target on the backs of you and your buddy Keys."

"Why is that?"

"Because, he was the catalyst for the riot, and you organized the guys after, preventing the authorities from gaining control. So, a word to the wise. You've been ratted on."

"Why are you telling me this?"

I owe you for what you did at the hole, and God, I'm glad he's back in there. Be careful." Then he moved on yelling, "Mail call!"

Maestro pondered what he just heard and filed it under "Special Attention to Be Given To," after he read his letter. When he opened the letter and removed it from the envelope, the two pictures inside fell out onto his lap. He laid the letter down and took a picture in each hand as he marveled at what he saw. There in his hands, for the first time for one, and the first time in years for the other, were his babies. They were both the most beautiful things he'd ever seen. He sat and grinned, marveled, and swelled with pride inside, causing him to fight back a tear. Then he laid them down beside him and retrieved the letter, very well written and filled with love. It began, Dear Father, which Maestro thought was very formal for a child of seventeen, but then she was a straight "A" student. The second part was more conventional, "Dear Daddy," in a hand that looked like it usually uses a crayon. So moved by what he read, he immediately responded with three letters. One to each of his children and one to Poo's mother, thanking her for the kindness shown to his eldest child, and for, finally, being honest with his youngest child. The fact that the letter confirmed his suspicions, that she was keeping him a secret from her, and withholding all the letters, would not get into this letter from fear of the way he would have expressed it. He sought to be civil, expressing only gratitude.

That being done, he turned his attention to the information given him by the guard that brought the mail, and decided that he should turn to the wisdom of war: prepare for battle in time of peace.

So, he got up, put his pictures and letters away, and began to stretch, meditate, and train. This would become a daily ritual.

The lock down lasted two months and two days. Letters from the kids came at least once a week, talking always of their developing relationship, and asking equally when he would make arrangements for them to come. He always wrote right back giving his best guess, which was usually something like, "It shouldn't be too much longer." On the second day, following the two month lock down, a Screw walked into the block and said in a loud voice, "In a few minutes, the doors to your cells will open. Every prisoner is instructed to proceed directly to the auditorium, where you'll all be addressed by the new Warden."

Then he left. Moments later, the doors opened and the guys rolled out. Having not seen each other for a couple of months, they began to congregate and talk. When the guard returned, he said, "Let's move out! Everyone must attend."

116

The first thing the guys noticed about the guards was that they were all outfitted with shoulder radios, handcuffs, night sticks, and gas canisters on their belts. The gas, cuffs, and night sticks, were all new, and only some of the guards used to have radios, now they all did. When they got to the auditorium, there were four high ranking Screws on the stage, flanking a man unknown to them in a dark blue suit.

A faint smell of death was still in the air. All the guards stood at attention, except the suit. He stood at ease, with his hands folded behind him. There was a P.A. system set up at the edge of the stage that awaited him when he was ready. When the guys were all present and seated, with the exception of those in the hole and the hospital, he approached the mic and spoke. "My name is simple and easy to remember. It's **WARDEN!**"

"This is now my prison, and what happened here will never happen again. At least, it will never happen on my watch. After the noon meal, we'll resume normal operations. I have been fully briefed on the functions of this facility. You will notice that the officers are now better prepared to defend themselves. You will also learn that you will no longer have access to anything that can be used as weapons, like candles, etc. You will no longer be in areas of this prison unsupervised." The list went on and on, and when he was done he said, "I'm not an unreasonable man, nor am I a foolish one. My door will be open to you and staff alike. As long as you can conduct yourselves accordingly, we can get things done. But trust me; you don't want to push me. It's not something you will win. Are there any questions?" There were none.

The men were then instructed to return to their cells, where they would remain until noon chow. The Warden did not need to say anything for them to get the message that the governor was willing to back him in mostly anything, as payback for signing and ordering the no reprisal for past deeds.

In the weeks to come the Screws tested their new found authorities, and often, not to mention their new toys: handcuffs and radios, mostly. But there were a few incidents where the clubs and gas were used. Most of that was done in the hole. On the up side, guys were allowed to resume their chosen activities. The band reassembled, and got back to creating their music. Kwanza was approaching, and the word came down that they could have their traditional event, which took place in the Visiting Center with family and friends. That meant that the band would play and the ceremony would be performed.

It was also a good opportunity for Maestro to arrange for his children to come. All the guys in the band that had family would invite them -Shot, Keys, Fingers included. They all knew Maestro got the green light to have his children come. He needed special permission for his, because they were both considered minors. But the eldest was close enough to eighteen for her to receive a pass, and she could bring her little sister with her.

So now the focus was on the performance, and they wanted it to be the best they had ever done. Keys was a little rusty, but determined not to let the gang down. They went to work, like men driven and determined.

Maestro wrote the letter that night, with the good news that they would finally see each other, and that he had a surprise for them when they did.

Kwanza being the celebration of people of African descent, the theme and style of music was already decided upon. Now, Maestro would be hard at work writing something that would make his children proud.

It was his only chance to make a good first impression, and he took it seriously. The rest of the guys knew how important this was to him, and would put their hearts into it, for all the right reasons. They had motivations because their families would be there too, and everyone could see their love for their music. Maestro was their friend and, of course, he was the head that had kept them alive through the riot. The new rules compelled them to endure a guard being posted in the Music Box during their rehearsals. His body language, during the first two rehearsals, told them just how rusty they were. But by the third one, the guard was starting to pat his feet, and by the next to the last rehearsal, he was cheering and applauding. His actions probably would not have gone over well with the new Warden or his peers, most of whom regarded prisoners as lesser people, if indeed, they considered them people at all. Someone even mentioned to the Screw that he may not want to take his excitement beyond the Music Box. He stuck out his chest and Said, "F" them; they knew it was for their benefit.

The guys were ready now and still had one rehearsal left. It would only be polish for the biggest event this prison ever saw. The music was right, the steps were glamorous, and the voices were razor sharp. Visiting room? Hell, they were ready for any stage in the world, but bathed in the knowledge that they were performing before the most important audience in the world: their families –The people who would love them more than any other, and long after others stopped. So it was fitting that they were at their best, for the sole purpose of giving their best to them. <u>WHO DESERVES MORE?</u>

When the kids got the letter, they read it together and began to jump and scream, saying, "We're going to see daddy, we're going to see daddy." Bones and her mother watched; Bones looked up at her mother and said, "Can I go see him too?" Her mother knew she could not say, "No" to this child who loved this man as much as she did her own father, and longer than Poo had been in the world.

She looked down at her and with a sigh simply said, "Y-e-a-h, we'll, all go." Bones lit up and ran to Poo and Pam and said, "I'm going, too, we all going." Then she ran back to her mother, hugged her and kissed her on the cheek and said, "Thank you, Mommy." Then she ran back to Poo and Pam and said, "We all going, Pam."

Pam looked down at her and smiled and said, "Cool." Everyone looked at Pam with this kind of, "when did you go from polite to hip?" look. Pam, looking kind of bewildered, said, "What?" Everyone looked at each other but no one said anything. Then Poo said, "Cool" with that grin of hers, and everyone burst into laughter. Then the girls went into this huddle and began talking about what they were going to wear. Mom was off to call Auntie again, as she thought, "I know she wants to hear this one."

The phone rang at Auntie's.

"Hello."

"Hey, girl. What's going on?"

"What's going on with you? You the one that made the call."

"Guess where I'm going?"

"Where? Crazy?"

"Nawh, girl. Prison."

"What! You finally shot Reggie?"

"No, I didn't shoot Reggie."

"Well, you should have."

"Stay with me, girl."

"Oh, you serious, huh?"

"Yeah, girl."

"Alright. Alright."

"Why you going to prison?"

"Poo's father invited the kids to an event, and Bones wants to go too. I can't say "no" to her. She loves him, too and wants to share that with her sister. And he loves her, too."

"Wow, girl! That's a kind of big one for you, huh?"

"Tell me about it."

"Well, that's part of the Mommy thing, right?"

"Yeah, it is."

"Anything I can do?"

"Now that you mention it, yeah. I could use some moral support."

"You want me to come to prison with you?"

Well, that's kind of the friendship thing, right?"

"Girl, if you need me, you know I'm there. When is it?"

"Saturday night."

"Saturday night! Girl, Denzel's on Saturday night. I can't make it."

"Girl, don't start."

"Ok, you know I'm just messing with you. Maybe we can see one of those riot things and be on T.V."

"Girl, you talking crazy now."

"It could happen."

"Maybe Denzel will be there too."

"Now you talking crazy."

"It could happen." They both began to giggle.

"I'll talk to ya later girl. And Sheila…"

"Yeah, thanks girl. I owe you big."

"No worries, girl. That's what friends are for, and I know you'd do it for me. Plus, it's for the kids and ya know I'm like you. I'd do anything for them."

"You're a good friend."

"Yeah, yeah, yeah."

They hung up.

## CHAPTER TWENTY-FOUR

Poo's and Pam's mother finally had that lunch about three months after the phone call. It began a little awkward as was to be expected, one would suppose. They spoke of how well each did their jobs as mothers, and how well-behaved their children were. Each took their turn praising their children and high-lighting what they thought were their children's best attributes. Then, Poo's mother broke the ice. "So how long were you two together?"

"Well, we knew each other only briefly, and were together in that way only once. The man went into the service the next day, and I never saw him again. We just lost touch, and time went on, as they say. I guess once was enough, huh? But I have no regrets. She's always been a joy to me. How about you?"

Poo's mother responded, "Well, we were together almost two years. It was good when it was good. We were happy, and then one night our whole life changed. Two guys attacked him one night in the parking lot of his job. One had a knife and one had one of those black jacks, and it got out of hand and he killed them both. When the smoke cleared, he was the one that went to prison. I know that if they would have killed him, they would not have gone to jail. It never occurred to anybody that they were destroying my daughter's and my life, too."

Pam's mother then said, "You sound like you really loved him, which is understandable, because he's very lovable." Poo's mother just said, "Uhmm." (But both understood that she meant more.)

Pam's mother went on to say: "You know, it's really none of my business, but if you still love him, then you should probably let him know."

Poo's mother simply said, "I think it's much too late for that."

Pam's mother asked, "Well, what does he think?"

Poo's mother responded, "I think he would agree."

Pam's mother said, coyly, "But you don't know?" (Their eyes met again.)

"I'm pretty sure," replied Poo's mother. "So, what do you do?"

"I work in a department store," answered Pam's mother.

"Are you married?"

"Yes. He's a good man, very supportive of me and my daughter" Pam's mother replied.

"No other kids?"

"Nope."

"By choice?" (Now, their eyes met again. This time there was sorrow in Pam's mother's.)

Poo's mother said, "I'm sorry, I don't mean to pry."

Pam's mother said, "No. No. It's okay. We're just talking. As a matter of fact, I did have another child, a son. He was killed when he was very young."

"I'm sorry."

"Thank you."

They took each other's hand and Pam's mother asked, "You got any brothers or sisters?"

"Just a best friend that's like a sister. I would like you to meet her sometime. She's really a dear person."

"Thanks, I would really like that."

"So how about you?"

"All brothers, four of them. Seems like that's all my mother and her sister chooses to have. My Aunt has four sons and one of them is Greg, the one who put Pam's father in touch with her."

Poo's mother smiled and said, "My husband supports Pam's relationship with him. I don't think he would support mine."

They both burst out laughing as the waiter arrived at the table and asked if they were ready to order. They did, and asked him to bring them a couple of cocktails while they waited for their meal. The waiter nodded and walked away. He was soon back at their side with the order. They sipped, they talked. They ate, they talked, and they laughed. They sipped, and they talked some more.

By the time they were ready to go, they couldn't wait to do it again. They had agreed that the man had good taste in his choice of "Ladies."

## CHAPTER TWENTY-FIVE

The day had arrived, and the Visiting Center was arranged in a supper club style. A small stage was assembled for the band. The equipment had been moved into place, set up, and fine-tuned. The guys took a sound check that afternoon, before anyone had arrived. So now, with their clothes laid out, everyone headed for the showers. Everyone agreed to dress in coal-black, for uniformity. Final checks were made on the refreshments, clearance for visitors, and the camera-man. Everyone had their instructions. They would meet together before it was time to go, form a circle, and take a quiet moment to reflect and encourage each other. They needed no motivation because the collective adrenaline would overload a lightning storm. But they would use it to do what they do best. Now, it was time to head for the Visiting Center. The guests from the world were allowed to enter the visiting room first. The tables all had name tags on them so that they could find their places; and now, the prisoners were allowed to find them. Of course, the band's families were sitting up front, since they were the ones to set up the Visiting Center. Everyone began to make their way through the Visiting Center to find their family and friends. When Keys rolled in, his son saw him first, and shouted, "Grandma, there's Daddy!" Shot, whose daughters hadn't seen him in about two years, screamed, "Daddy!" and came running. Maestro saw his table, and much to his surprise, it was full. Breathing an inner sigh of relief that they had made it, he began to make his way to his table, noticing that its occupants started turning their heads in search of him, and making each other aware that he was on his way. When he got to the table, he saw the two beautiful children in the picture, and then noticed they were not alone. His eldest daughter rose first to greet him with a warm hug saying, "You look just like your picture."

He stepped back and said, "Let me look at you. You're beautiful." He then looked over at Poo and said, "You're getting to be a big girl, aren't-cha?"

She showed him that million dollar smile which melted him, and he swept her off her feet, and gave her a big hug. He placed her on his hip and turned to face the rest of the table finding Poo's mother rising to greet him. There she was, an inch shorter than himself. She wore a dark brown dress, which rested just above her knees, with three strokes of white in it, which played perfectly against her caramel complexion. Her dress hugged her body just enough to reveal all the right curves, topped with a dimpled flank smile, that reminded him why he was so attracted to her when they first met. Her black shoulder length hair was swirled into bangs that fell over one eye. She wore a small heel, opened toe shoe, which revealed a fresh pedicure to match a fresh manicure.

Surprised to see her, (face showing it), "Hello, Leitha", (she cutting him off), "Your letter of thanks was warm and friendly, and Bones wanted to come, too. She could only get in if I came."

Maestro knew it was so. Even though he loved her as if she was his own, he knew the rules would not let her come with Pam, because she wasn't blood.

He gazed down at her and said, "Hey, you. You're becoming quite a young lady. You're gonna break a lot of hearts."

She smiled shyly and said, "Hi!"

He said, "Hi! You better come over here and give me a hug." She did. Leitha said, "You remember Sheila (Auntie), right?"

"Yeah, of course. How you, side-kick?" Maestro said with grin.

"Fine, how you Black Panther?" Sheila returned with her own grin. Maestro still grinning, said, "Touché, good one," and they both hugged. Sheila then said, "Are we gonna see inside, like where y'all do y'all's riots?" Maestro said, "Not unless you plan to stay for a few years." Sheila said, "Nope. I'm fine. I like my freedom too much." Maestro said, "Yeah, I like you having your freedom too." They smiled at each other and Sheila sat down. Then Maestro turned to Leitha again, who was clearly nervous, and took her by both hands and kissed her on the cheek and said, "How have you been?"

"I'm okay, I guess."

"Thanks for coming, I missed seeing Bones and Poo."

She playfully said, "And how about me?"

He just smiled and said, "Why don't we all sit down." Then the guys came over and introduced their families. Maestro proudly introduced everyone at the table as his daughters, and their mother, and her side-kick, with a smile that let everyone at the table know what he meant, but none of the other's unless they knew his family.

His peers also exchanged brief hellos. Then the guys said, "Nice meeting you all," to the families, and said to Maestro, "We'll see ya in a minute." The ten went to the bandstand to begin their set, which consisted of jazz tunes and other instrumentals. Lou (whose family was from out-of-state), stayed behind, and said to Sheila, "It was especially nice to meet you." She smiled shyly and said, "Thank you, it was nice to meet you, too." Lou said, in that deep voice of his, "I don't wish to intrude but do you mind if I join you?" Sheila said, "Not at all, if no one else minds." No one objected. He sat, they talked, she giggled occasionally, like a schoolgirl and he blushed occasionally, like a schoolboy. They were making a night of it.

At one point, Maestro cleared his throat and said to Sheila and Lou, "Would you two like to be alone?" All of the adults at the table got a little chuckle out of it, and Lou said, "Naw, Bro, we're fine, aren't we?" with his arm now around Sheila's chair. Sheila said in a schoolgirl kind of way, "Don't cha just love his voice?" Maestro, with a kind of warm and sincere smirk, simply said, "I think it's enough for my friend that you love it."

Leitha said (with a grin on her face) "Whatever makes you happy, girl. No offense, is it Lou?"

Lou said, "Yes," and went on to say, "I'm not offended. Most of my life my voice has been a point of interest for somebody." Maestro said, "Yeah, I'm one of the witnesses to that." And he and Lou looked at each other and smiled with Lou saying, "Don't start man." The ladies said, "What's up with that?" The guys looked at each other, grinned and said at the same time, "Private joke." Then they chuckled. The ladies looked at each other and just kind of hunched their shoulders, as if to say, "Whatever."

The kids asked Daddy, "What's the surprise?"

He said, "That's my band and you're going to see me perform."

Poo said, "You're going up there, daddy?"

"Yes."

"For what?" (Everyone broke into laughter) He grabbed her and pulled her to him. She screamed and laughed harder, and he said, "I see you're still ticklish."

Pam said, "I saw a picture of you with a band. Is this them? They're good."

"They're the best."

"You sing?"

"Yes. Do you have any talents for this?"

"Well, I'm a music lover, does that count?"

He chuckled and kissed her on the forehead and said, "Yeah, that counts."

Maestro had written two of the songs they were to perform, one was about Kwanza, and one was about freedom. They spent the time getting to know each other, and Maestro with his wits would occasionally bring them all to laughter. He was conscious to include everyone in the conversation. As the band played on people began to rock and pat their feet. Family members of the band would occasionally shout things like, "Play ya'll, Play!" Some would say, "That's my daddy!" Some would say, "That's my man!" Maestro's table was rocking and bopping. In the midst of the funky jam, the drums rolled, and Keys raised his hand and dropped it. With it, came down the sound of the band almost to a whisper. Then he stepped from behind the key boards and walked to the center mic, then said, "Good evening, Ladies and Gentlemen." Maestro thinking out loud said, "Here we go!" Keys went on as Poo climbed down, to everybody's surprise, turned her chair around so that the back faced the stage, causing everyone to examine what appeared to be strange behavior. She then climbed back up on the seat with her knees in the chair, folded her arms across the top and rested her chin on her arms. She now had a ring side seat. Mom raised an eyebrow in amazement as Keys went on, "Thank you all for joining us this evening, we have a very special performance planned for you in light of not only the occasion, but also the history in the house tonight. So without any further delay, let me bring forth five of the baddest men that ever did it. Please put your hands together and meet, greet, and show your love for the Old School Brotherhood." The music went up and Keys found his place, and applause brought the five to the stage. Sheila commented that Lou was kind of sexy.

Maestro stepped back to face the band, then turned to join the ranks, and took center stage. As he did, the music came to an abrupt halt. He said, "Dear families of all, and mine in particular, on behalf of the Old School Brotherhood Family, we want you to know, that (now joined by the other four in harmony)"There's music in the house tonight." Three of the singers reached for the sky and the other two reached for the ground, on the down beat of the drum, and then the reverse.

The audience "Exploded," and so did the stage. They were off bringing the house down already, and it would keep getting better with every new tune, and each new step. The songs of freedom and Kwanza featured leads from all the group members, and filled the audience with pride and tears.

The electricity on the stage was felt by all, and the fellas knew that their preparation was complete. They could do no wrong. They probably couldn't make a mistake if they tried. That's how hard they had worked for this. The set ended with a standing ovation that surpassed the first four numbers. Afterwards, they would take a break for the Kwanza ritual and spend some time with their families. All the tables were buzzing about the performance that they just witnessed, and for this night, everyone would enjoy celebrity status. Sticks' (the Spanish brother on the timbales) family came all the way from the Dominican Republic for this occasion, and were glad that they did. Shot's daughters were over in the corner with him giggling and attempting to mock his dance steps. Maestro's daughters were beaming, as Pam said, "You guys are really, really good!"

Poo weighed in, "Yeah, daddy. Ya'll gonna do some mo?"

Maestro answered, "Maybe later sweetheart."

"Alright," she said with a little bop that made everyone laugh.

Bones asked, "You write those songs, daddy?" causing everyone to turn and take note of the fact that she addressed him as "daddy", but he took it in stride, having enjoyed this honor when she was younger. Everyone else joined suit, and played it the same way.

"Yes, I wrote two of them and co-wrote one."

Pam spoke, "You can make a lot of money doing that, you know. You all are better than a lot of the groups out there."

"Thanks for the vote of confidence, sweetheart."

Mommy asked Sheila to take the kids to the table that was set up in the back, and bring back refreshments for everyone. Sheila knew she wanted a moment alone, and said, "Sure. Come on ya'll."

Then, Mommy turned to Maestro and said, "The kids are right. You are good."

"Thanks."

"Are you okay with me being here?"

"Yeah. It's just that it's been a long time and you took me by surprise."

"Touché. I guess I should apologize for that, but I didn't even have your new number so I could warn you."

'It's okay. It worked out."

"But us, will we ever get to talk?"

"I suppose. I just don't know if tonight is the best time."

"Oh, I know. I'm not saying tonight. I was just wondering in general."

"So, are you seeing anyone?" He looked at her as if to say "Don't lie"

"No. Not at the moment." (Being reminded of the betrayal, and guilt, showed as a result.)

He said, in an attempt to ease her, "You've done a great job with the kids. They look great. But you were always a great mother."

"Thanks."

"So, how's your Mother?"

"Oh, she's fine. She wanted me to say 'hello' for her."

"Tell her I said, hi."

Now the kids were back with fruit and pastries. Bones not bothering to take her seat, walked behind maestro, stuck her fingers between his collar bone and neck and said, "You remember this?" Maestro tensed up and went into convulsion-type laughter. He used to tickle her that way. He grabbed her and said, "Yeah, I remember. You?" And did the same thing to her and got the same results. Then he went for the other two. "Ya'll ticklish, too?" They began their fit before he even touched them, but it didn't stop him. Pam bolted, and almost ran from the table to get out his reach. Then she crept back slowly, making him promise not to get her again. Looking very devilishly, he did and added, "You don't trust me."

She said, "Daddy, please," in a way that was begging.

He said, "You're safe. You can come back." He still had a hold on Bones and Poo.

They were all having fun when Maestro reached up and grabbed their mother, who had a similar reaction to Pam. When the kids discovered that she too was vulnerable, they went after her. She fought them off, while Maestro turned his attention back to Pam.

"So, how's school?"

"Good."

"What do you hope to be?"

"A lawyer!"

"Oh yeah! What motivated this?"

"I want to help you get out of prison."

He was touched by the statement. Poo overhearing, turned and crashed the conversation saying, "Daddy, when you coming home? You gonna live with us?"

Mommy and Maestro's eyes met at that moment, and Maestro returned his attention to Poo saying, "You sure got a lot of questions, don't you." She shook her head "yes" and he laughed and said, "Come with me to light a Kwanza candle." She put her hand in his and they were off to the table where the ceremony had begun. Mom looked on with relief that they finally were together, father and daughter, and no one had gotten cussed out. Pam and Bones just kind of took in the surroundings. They returned to the table and Maestro asked, "Is everyone enjoying themselves?" He visually checked each one, including their mother, for signs of enjoyment. They all professed to be. A tug on Maestro's pants made him look down to find Poo nodding and saying, "Yeah, me too," making it unanimous and bringing laughter from everyone. The band started up again and played a couple of numbers. Then the audience began to chant, "Bring on Old School Brotherhood, Bring on Old School Brotherhood." Keys found his way again to the mic saying, "We aim to please. So once more, give it up for. . . .", and the joint blew up again in anticipation. And before they were done they had lived up to and surpassed all expectations. They had touched every emotion and every soul. This night would come up in conversations, inside and out, for some time to come. At the end of the evening, Maestro took his family into a group hug, took a picture with them, and told them that there is never enough time. But if they loved him as he did them, then they would love each other and always stay close to one another. He took each of the children, one by one and told them of his love for them, how proud he was of them, how much he enjoyed seeing them and how high his hopes were of seeing them again, vowing soon to be in touch before then. Pam promised to return soon and promised to bring Poo, to which Maestro responded how much he would look forward to it. He hugged them all very affectionately, and turned to Leitha, took her into his arms for a warm and gentle hug. She bathed in the moment, remembering. He stepped back and said as he placed a finger under her chin to tilt it upwards, "We'll talk soon okay?"

"Okay."

He kissed her again on the cheek and then gave her another hug saying, "Thank you for this night. I won't forget it."

She felt as she walked off and waved, that she had taken a step to right past wrongs, and that made her feel real good.

Before they were at the door, to the surprise of everyone, Lou took Sheila in his arms and said, "I really enjoyed your company this evening and hope we will have another." Sheila said, "I will look forward to it." They smiled at each other and shared a quick kiss on the lips. Mom got caught with her mouth opened and Maestro raised an eyebrow. Sheila said, "Take care, Lloyd", as she slowly moved away from Lou with the rest of the group moving with her. Maestro and Lou stood together and waved. Maestro looked at Lou and said, "Well, alright then." Lou, with a sheepish grin, said, "Y-e-a-h."

They were at the door about to leave when Poo bolted and ran back for a final hug. Mommy knew in her heart that it should never have taken this long for her baby to get that hug. She also knew that she would do whatever was necessary from here on out to honor their bond and whatever was possible beyond that, she would also be open to.

This night would be the beginning of the future. What it holds would be anybody's guess. But yesterday, every door seemed closed. So if nothing else, this was progress, even for Sheila.

## CHAPTER TWENTY-SIX

The car buzzed on the way home. Everyone had a great time, and everyone had great memories and new expectations. Mommy, with her arms around the girls, addressed questions from them. Like Poo saying, "Mommy, do you love my daddy?" "Yes, Poo," with Bones chiming in, "Do you love my daddy, too?"

Mommy replying, "I was lucky enough to be in love twice, and twice blessed because I have both of you. So, you see even if love don't last, love can be good and what comes of it can last. You understand?" Bones replied, "Yes, Mommy." They both looked at Poo, who was paying attention. She just nodded, "Yes," also.

Meanwhile, back at the, (I won't go there) prison, Maestro and the crew were beaming themselves, when they got back to the block.

Maestro took his time to express his gratitude to each and every member of the group. He was never more pleased with them. Even some of the Screws commented on how great they had been. The days and weeks that followed revealed that, that night had brought a lot of families closer together, not just for the band members like Keys, Shot, Maestro and Sticks, but for many, many others who were present at the event. All of the guys had seen their families several times since then, including Maestro. He had even spoken with both of his daughters' mothers by phone.

It was now spring and the trees were blooming, flowers were budding and Father's Day was on the way. Things were going so well that even though it was springtime, they were seeing temperatures of 101 degrees.

Maestro's daughters wanted their father all to themselves on Father's Day. So they began planning for that day six weeks in advance. Dad had only done two shows for the population, making room for the other bands to do their thing. The "Joint" had its ups and downs, but nothing major. Then one day early in June, one of those 101 degree days, Key's mother and son set out to visit him. A three hour ride of buses and trains, and a quarter of a mile walk up the road from the bus stop in the blazing sun, brought them to the prison door, where she was greeted by one of the Screws that never forgave prisoners for the riot. He informed her that her slip was showing and as a result, Key's mother was not allowed to enter the prison on that day.

Her grandson, with his innocent eyes, looked up at his grandmother and said, "We can't see Daddy?" Grandmother pleaded with the officers to allow them to enter, but they were callous and disrespectful. The actions applied to this lady of great respect and years, well past eighty, were uncalled for, and undoubtedly, witnessed by other visitors who were passing by.

Overtaken by the heat, the mother requested a drink of water, which she was refused. The reason cited was that she was not allowed to enter that day. One Screw even went as far as saying, "Try us tomorrow. The water will be even colder and then you will enjoy it more." All the guards had a good chuckle about that. With her hanky in one hand, and her grandson holding the other, she turned away to begin the long journey home. Half way down the hill, and overwhelmed by the heat, and the stress of the humiliation she had just endured, her heart failed her and she collapsed and died on the road. Her grandson, too young to know what to do, just sat with her body, and cried until another visitor came up the road some forty-five minutes later, and informed the authorities. When the authorities learned of what had happened, they knew that it would be a problem. They went and got Keys and took him to the "Hole." They would say that it was, "For his own safety," then they gave him the bad news, and he "Flipped out." He was told that his son was with Social Services and they would track down his mother, which only added to Key's state of mind.

He wanted out. He wanted a phone call, and he wanted to see the Warden. What he got was arrogance and rules that made no sense. He even got laughed at, and one officer made the statement, "When our brothers were being beaten and killed because of you last year, who gave them a phone call, let them see the Warden, or let them out!"

"I have no sympathy for you," said the officer and they left Keys there alone, in the darkness, and stench of the "Hole." All Keys could do was scream, and he did, over and over again.

Ordinarily, the other guys in the "Hole" would be hollering, "Shut the F Up," but they heard the craziness that Keys just dealt with and gave him his time to work some of the pain out of his system. The word spread quickly from the Visiting Center through the whole Joint, and while no one said so, they expected Maestro to address the matter in some way. But Maestro did not need any invitation; Keys was a friend, band member, and therefore, family. He requested to see the Warden with a couple of the other guys. The Warden's position was clear and unyielding. He would stand behind his men, and not second guess them; that was all. The next day they learned that Keys had been transferred to the "Prison's Nut House," where he was sure to be in a strait jacket and constantly medicated, in an attempt by officials to avoid liability. They had gotten away with this sort of thing before, many times in the past. The position was, "You don't fix what ain't broken." Keys was lost to them, and Maestro, hearing the warning of the mail officer in his mind, could not help feeling one down, and me to go...

Keys, as a result of the drugs, was in a catatonic state. He was aware of his surroundings, but could not participate in them. The prison rules stated that if a prisoner lost a family member, they could elect to go either to the wake or funeral, or when possible, to the death bed, to say good-byes, as long as it was in the same state they were imprisoned in. Because they had drugged Keys into this condition he was now in, they made the decision for him and elected the wake. They arrived while the service was in progress and interrupted it by shouting upon entry to the Funeral home, "Clear the way! Clear the way! Prisoner coming through. Official business, do not interfere. Everyone remain seated. We won't be here long."

The audience was shocked, as they marched in with Keys in shackles, waist and legs. The priest cleared his throat loudly, trying to hint to them to give the service its proper respect. But they ignored him, shotguns hoisted and mounted on their hips, side-irons on display in full uniform, as they walked right up to the casket and said to Keys, with all the authority they could put in a statement, "You got two minutes, prisoner." And then took one step back away from him and began to look around as if to say to the on-lookers, "Don't try anything." Keys, aware of the moment, was powerless to even speak in his state, to apologize to family and friends for this outrage, and blatant display of disrespect. He could only unleash the tears of loss and rage.

He spoke to his mother with his heart and begged her to forgive him for the madness she had faced because she loved him. His son left the grips of relatives and went to Keys, one of the guards placed his hand out to stop the child, and an uncle rose. The guard placed his free hand on the pump part of the shotgun and was about to level it in the uncle's direction, when his wife spoke and said very softly, "It's his son. What's the harm?"

The guard felt all eyes on him now, and looked to his partner for a sign of what to do. His partner tilted his head towards Keys, as if to say go ahead. The guard allowed the child to pass. Keys' son went to him and simply took his hand. Keys knew he was there, but the drugs had him paralyzed. He could only stare. But for some strange reason his son seemed to understand. They looked at each other, hand in hand, and then just stared at the coffin together. Then the voice came again, "Time's up, prisoner." They stepped forward, took Keys by the arms and escorted him out, the same way they brought him in. His son watched as they removed his father, and turned back to face his grandmother's coffin, as if to say, "I will stand in for my father."

## CHAPTER TWENTY-SEVEN

The mood of the joint changed severely, and the Screws were out of control. They were arrogant, abusive, and backed by their leader, the new Warden. There were similar incidents to Keys' happening: guards getting the names and addresses of prisoners' wives and girlfriends, through their visiting cards, and calling them, harassing them and even a few rapes had occurred. If this was not enough, after an assault on a family member, the prisoner of that family member would be threatened to be quiet or further incidents would continue. There was a large increase in prisoner murders, but ruled out as suicides. The walls were closing in and no official was lifting a finger to stop it. Some of the media were sympathetic, but had no proof.

The sun rose on Father's Day, and Maestro began his ritual of meditation, stretching and training. When the yard opened after breakfast, he would go for his five mile run and then come back and stretch some more. He would then shower and groom himself for the anticipated visit from his children that was planned six weeks earlier. He joined the fellows for the noon chow, but gave most of it away, except for the milk and fruit. He went back to his cell to dress and await their arrival. At the stroke of one o'clock, they began to announce the list of names and prison numbers of those who had received visits thus far – a list of maybe twenty names. Maestro was not one of them. Flashbacks of Keys' mother and son being turned away, and her lying on that road, with her grandson crying over her body, began to haunt him. Keys, his only crime that he loved and mourned his mother got him sentenced to "Nut City." That began to anger Maestro. He took a deep breath and put his rage away. The same rage, now intensified, had brought him to this house of madness. As his mind began to drift back to that night, he began to hear another series of names and numbers being shouted out by the officers. His was the seventh one called.

He left his cell, bumping into Shot and Lou, who were on their way to wish him a good one. Closer to the Visiting Center he ran into Greg. Greg asked him to send a message to his family by way of Maestro's daughter. Maestro assured him that he would not forget.

Unknown to Maestro at the time, one of the officers out front had given Poo a piece of candy which Poo had put into her mouth as she entered the Visiting Center. Maestro entered the Visiting Center behind two other prisoners and the Screw pulled the door behind him shut. They all stopped at the desk to check in. As they did and proceeded to step away, they slowed, seemingly startled by something they saw. Maestro could hear a commotion of some kind and someone falling and someone screaming. He heard the whimper of a child's voice, as if with their last breath, saying "Help me, Daddy. Help me!" As the two men in front of Maestro stepped away towards their own visits, Maestro's view to the disturbance was clear and there in the center of the visiting room, his eldest daughter laid on the floor dazed, and his baby's feet were dangling in the air five feet off the floor with some Screw's hands around her throat. He was screaming, "Spit it out...I said spit it out!" For a split second, time seemed to go in slow motion. There was a Screw between Maestro and the attacker of his child, and there was a Screw behind him, who had let him in and was busy locking the door back. The Screw turned just in time to see Maestro's eyes lock, spill a tear, and display rage within a second. Maestro started towards the attacker, who had his back towards him. The Screw stepped into his path and raised his hand like a traffic cop, while pushing the emergency button on his belt with his other hand and said, "Hold it right there!"

Now the Screw in the rear of him was hurrying towards him, but Maestro never broke stride. He fired a right palm at the Screw, driving his nose into his brain. With the same motion, he brought his elbow back into the forehead of the Screw behind him, causing the Screw to stagger back, just far enough for Maestro to get off a back jab kick that crushed the Screw's windpipe. The Screw who had his daughter, looked over his shoulder just in time to see his co-workers die, and panicked, slinging Poo and attempting to run while screaming, "You stay away from me!" Maestro caught him from behind, the same way he had Poo. Using the momentum of his running, he snatched him off his feet into a swirl, much like some maniac fathers do with their children when they pick them up by the ankles and twirl them. But Maestro had the Screw by the neck, and as soon as his feet were level with the rest of his body in the air, Maestro lowered the Screw's neck, and twisted, causing gravity and the weight of his body to team up on the neck and snap it like a twig; a snap that echoed throughout the Visiting Center. When Maestro heard the snap, he just let go. The mangled body just dropped like a rag doll.

Maestro ran to his children and helped Poo first. She was coughing, her eyes were red and watering, and she was also shaken. But beyond that, she was alright and very glad to see her father. She wrapped her arms around his neck and held on for dear life. Maestro crouched down with just a kind of duck position, walked over to his eldest child, who was starting to rise saying, "You see what they did to us, Daddy?" Maestro responded, "Yeah, they won't ever do that again!" Just then he heard the pump action of a shotgun behind him and a voice that said, "Freeze!"

With his children still in his embrace, he looked over his shoulder. The visitors were frozen, and in shock at what they had just seen. There stood three Screws with guns, one with a shotgun and two with pistols. This was the Warden's new "Elite Squad," to take care of matters beyond the capacity of his regular Screws, and they were gung-ho. They ordered Maestro to stand up, raise his hands where they could see them, and step away from the children. Other

Screws had started to arrive by then, and began to move the prisoners and their visitors against the far walls.

Maestro told Pam to take Poo and take care of her, as he passed Poo into Pam's extended arms. Maestro kissed them both and told them, "Don't worry. You'll be alright!"

Then Maestro stood up and moved to the center of the floor with his hands up, looking the armed guards right in their eyes fearlessly. The Screw with the shotgun, also the nearest and the only one that spoke since entering the Visiting Center, raised the shotgun and said, "Step Forward."

His raising the shotgun must have panicked Poo, because Poo broke away from Pam' s hold and ran towards Maestro yelling, "Daddy!" Her sudden movement panicked the guard with the shotgun, causing him to swing it towards her. Maestro, with what only could be described as a trained father's instinct screamed, "No!" and what looked like the speed of light, jumped and threw a spin kick into the Screw, and the Screw with the shotgun, was dead before he hit the ground.

Then there was darkness. Poo began to scream, "You killed my Daddy! You killed my Daddy!" She kicked the guard she was closest to in the shins, and he raised his hand to backhand her, when Pam ran up grabbing Poo, and screamed, "You better not touch her, you bastard!" The guard said, "What did you say?"

Before Pam could answer, a voice was heard from the crowd of visitors saying, "You heard what she said!" Then the rest of the visitors began to speak and move up behind Poo and Pam, saying things like "That's right! That's enough of this shit. Get the man some help, move now. "

Just then a captain came in, and made his way to the center of the room where Maestro laid. He ordered the guards to roll back and told the crowd that help was on the way. By now Poo and Pam were on their knees by their father. The captain wanted them to step back, but they would not move and the crowd insisted, "Leave them alone."

Maestro woke up three days later in the prison ward of an outside hospital, chained by the ankles to the bed with a nurse standing over him saying, "It was touch and go for a minute there, but they got both the bullets out."

Maestro said, "Where. How's my children?"

The nurse, looking a bit confused, said, "You're from the Prison, aren't you? That's why you're on this ward."

Maestro asked, "Could I get a phone to make a call?" The nurse told him that she would get the doctor.

The doctor came in to find Maestro in an agitated state and said to Maestro, "Calm down, you're going to live and you'll be fine."

Maestro began to speak, and the doctor cut him off saying, "There is also someone here to see you, but she can only stay a minute because you're considered "High Security. "Plus you need your rest!"

The doctor waved, and Poo's mother came through the door. Maestro only got Poo, out of his mouth and her mother cut him off and said, "She's fine. They're both fine. But she thinks it's her fault that you got shot."

"You tell her, nothing is her fault."

"I have," Poo's mother told Maestro. "Pam is pretty shaken up, and feeling like it was her fault. She says she let you down. Something about she was to keep Poo, and she let her get away from her."

"You tell my children that I love them both very much, and that I blame them for nothing, and they are not to blame themselves either. I am just happy that they are alright," Maestro responded with relief.

"Do you need anything?" Poo's mother asked.

'No. I just need to know that everyone is alright." Poo's mother then told Maestro, "It's been on the news. They are going to charge you with four counts of murder, when you get better."

"I expect as much, and some more stuff. But they can't have our babies." Maestro responded with dignity in his voice.

Poo's mother smiled at the inclusion, and said, "They won't let me stay. I've got to go, but I'll try to come again, if they let me." Then she leaned down and kissed Maestro on the lips.

Maestro looked up and said, "What's that for?"

"Uumm, call it for saving the kids. See ya, bye."

When she walked out, the Warden was walking in and did a double take on her, and then said to the nurse, "He is not to have any visitors."

The nurse said to him, "I don't make those decisions, sir. You'll have to take that up with the hospital administrators."

The Warden looked at the nurse coldly and responded, "I will," and when he turned and faced Maestro, the nurse now standing behind the Warden, winked, then left.

The Warden said, "You killed four of my officers, you are now considered the most dangerous convict in my prison. As soon as you are medically cleared, you will be charged with these murders and you will spend the rest of your days in the hole!"

Maestro never spoke a word. He just listened, and then closed his eyes, and went on to sleep. Probably just to make sure he wasn't dreaming. ...

The Warden returned to the prison and immediately called a meeting of all his top command. He was raving, "Why did I not know about this guy? I have four dead officers and four grieving families. The press is up my ass, and the Goddamn Governor is calling me every five minutes. Why the hell didn't I know how dangerous this man is? Somebody answer me!"

"Sir, while you were at the hospital, this came in. After the story broke all over the news, I guess the State Department decided to contact the Commissioner. He is one of the best trained Special Forces. He was in Vietnam for six years. He went on rescue missions behind enemy lines eight times, three of them by himself, and never lost a man."

The Warden says, "Now I find this shit out. Heads are going to roll. Who fucked with him anyway?" No one dared answer that question.

## CHAPTER TWENTY-EIGHT

Maestro awoke again, still in the prison ward, but the Warden was gone. Amid the drugs, he tried to take in the surroundings. There were your assorted stabbings, broken bones, nut cases that had attempted suicide. On one side of Maestro, there was one such case. This guy looked at Maestro and said, "You should have killed them all. They're not going to let you get away with it anyway."

Then the guy blurted out, "They raped me, and I had to get stitches. You should've killed them all."

On the other side of Maestro was a burn victim. Someone had boiled some water, put jelly in it to make it stick, and threw it on him. Apparently, he was the bully in the prison he was from; an angry man, and cynical.

The man said, "He's right, you know. You should have killed them all. They are only going to send you some rookie lawyer to sell you out."

Just as he said that, Maestro heard a voice that said, "I assure you that I am neither a rookie, nor am I here to sell you out." Maestro turned to see a guard, and one of the most beautiful women he had ever laid eyes on. She was coconut brown and had long braids like an African Queen, which reminded him of Poo. She was taller than him, and had long slender, but firm, legs.

Maestro said, "They sent you to woo me?"

"No, to defend you."

The guard looked at her, and grunted, then said, "And you asked for this case? Good luck, mouthpiece." Then turned and left.

She never acknowledged him. She just stood looking at Maestro.

Maestro then said, "Okay, if you're not some rookie, you will earn my apology, and if you're not a sellout, then you will earn my undying gratitude."

She glanced over at the burn victim who made the comment as she was walking into the room, then pulled the curtain around Maestro's bed area, sealing off other viewers. She pulled up a chair beside Maestro's bed, and introduced herself.

"My name is Shanon Harris, and I will be representing you in this matter." Then she extended her hand to Maestro.

Maestro shook it, while studying her for clues of what she was about. She went on to say, "I know these are not the best conditions

157

for privacy, but they are going to charge you with "Four Counts of First Degree Murder," and I need your side of the story."

Maestro told her the facts as he remembered them. When he was done, she said, "The medical report says you took two gun shots, one to the shoulder and one to the lower chest, both of which entered through the back. Were you running or walking away at the time?"

"No. The last thing I remember was him pointing that shotgun at my child."

"Okay, that will be all for now. They will be doing a bedside arraignment tomorrow. I'll try to keep you here as long as I can. I know you're in no hurry to go to the hole; especially, in your condition. You know they're not feeling very friendly towards you, or me for that matter. So, rest and I'll see you tomorrow."

Then she got up, returned the chair, opened the curtain, and was on her way out. When she reached the door, Maestro hailed her. "Hey!" She turned, and he said, "Why?" A look of confusion came over her face, and she said, "Why? Why, what?"

"Why did you ask for this case?"

With just a hint of sarcasm and a touch of a smirk she said, "Why else, to earn your undying gratitude, of course." Then she disappeared through the door.

The next day Maestro was awakened by the doctor, who checked his vital signs, and then said, "You're going to be moved into one of the side rooms that just opened up, and there're some people here to see you."

Maestro was moved, and then his attorney entered with a stenographer, D.A., and a Judge, following her. The attorney spoke first saying, "How are you feeling today?" Maestro never spoke. She went on to say, "Like I told you yesterday, these people are here to arraign you." Then she stood by his bed and faced the others, extending her hand, palm up, indicating to them to proceed. The D.A. began:

"You're charged with the following indictments, charging you with four counts of First Degree Murder. How do you plead?"

Before Maestro could speak, his attorney stated, "My client pleads "Not Guilty" to all counts."

They went through other legal formalities, and then they were gone. The attorney told Maestro, that they would be coming at him quickly, and they will be playing hard ball. "If there is anything that you can tell me that will help, let me know. I'll be on call for you twenty-four hours a day until this is over. I have left my number with the nurse, to call at your request, and I am leaving my card on your night stand. One more thing you should know. I hate losing. The only thing I hate more than that is losing to the government. So please, I beg you to always be straight with me, no matter what. Okay?"

Maestro nodded because now she started to speak his language. She was about to leave, but Maestro said, "Wait, I think I know where you can start. I don't know how it will play on this matter, but there is a tape you should see."

"Well, let me be the judge of that. Where's the tape?"

"Take down this number and tell them I said it's okay to give you a copy."

"I'll have my investigator get right on it."

He gave her a look of surprise, with a hint of suspicion. She said, "Don't worry, I trust these people with my life."

"Now you're trusting them with mine?"

"You must learn not to worry so much."

"Why?"

"Because you've got me on your side." She sent the investigator after the tape, and she went to visit his daughters to get their side of the events.

Poo, with her mother by her side, told the lawyer that, "A man hit my sister and was choking me, and my daddy made him stop. Then they shot him, because he wouldn't let them shoot me." Shanon thought she was great. Then she said to Poo's mother, "I never wish to put a child through that ordeal, but I might need her to testify for him."

"I don't know about that. She's kind of young, and I don't want people beating up on her."

"I understand your concern. You don't have to decide anything now. Just think about it."

Poo said, "What's Testy-why?"

They both laughed and Shanon touched her on the nose, and said, "You're too much." Then she asked Poo's mother for some background on Maestro.

"I don't really know what I can tell you. We've been out of touch for years."

"Tell me about him when you were together."

"Well, listen, you want some coffee?"

"Sure, that would be nice." And they went there.

Shanon's next stop was the prison, to visit Shot, who gave her a run-down, not only on Maestro, but the system. She asked, "Is there staff around here we can trust?"

"No! Oh, wait! He and that Screw that hands out the mail are kind of civil with each other. But I wouldn't put much stock in him."

"Why?"

"Cause he's a Screw. He's one of them. You're his lawyer and you haven't figured that out?"

"Calm down, I'm figuring things out all the time. I figured out that I don't have a prisoner's vantage point, and I figured I should talk to you. So, don't count me out yet. Now, is there any more you can tell me? Someone else I should see maybe?"

"No, ahh, not that I can think of."

"Okay, thank you for your time."

"Hey!"

"Yes?"

"Let him know that all the guys are pulling for him, will ya?"

"Sure, if you let the guys know I'm pulling for him, too."

"Deal."

They shook hands and she was out. She chose to get the investigator to get the 411 (information) on the mail officer, away from the prison. She would be right; in the meantime she would check the tape this investigator had dropped off. While she finished up the tape, the investigator called in to say he had some good stuff and he taped it. He was also referred to another guard and was on his way to see him, and would be back in the office in a couple of hours.

This would give Shanon a chance to go see Pam and get her version. Then, make a quick stop at the coroner's. Later, back at the office, she and the investigator got together to compare notes. After going through all the stuff they had, and getting straight on their itinerary for the next day, they called it a day. That night as she lay awake in bed, Shanon marveled at the profile of Maestro, and actually looked forward to seeing him the next day. Everything from his military record to the way he did time, to the kind of father he tried to be, said he was a very principled man. She was troubled by the shape she found his eldest daughter in. She took the guilt of his injuries all on herself, feeling that she let him down badly, which depressed her and made her refuse to face him, out of shame. This isn't something Shanon wanted to report to Maestro, because she knew he was more concerned about his children than himself. She feared this would only distract him, and the trial date was close.

The next morning, after getting little sleep, Shanon showered, got dressed, had coffee, and was off to the prison ward. Today was the day Maestro would get his stitches out and she knew she would not be able to keep him in the hospital much longer. It would be back to the joint once more, specifically the "Hole," and she would have to deal with the nonsense of misplaced paper work and the rest of the crap that comes along with one defending against the system.

Upon her arrival, Shanon found Maestro awake, sitting up, and stitches free. The first question he asked was, "Have you seen my children? Are they alright?"

Shanon lied and said, "They're both fine." Their eyes met and then they both looked away. Shanon then said, "Okay, the good news or, the bad news, which do you want first?"

163

"The bad," was all Maestro said.

"Well, the bad news is, I don't know how much longer I can insist that you stay here."

Maestro said, "What else?"

"That's it for the bad news. The good news is we are going to give them the fight of their life. You are quite a remarkable man."

"There's nothing special about me. I'm just a man like any other man!"

"Be that as it may, you had the foresight to make that tape, and you made quite an impression on a couple of guards. Plus, we got some good stuff in discovery. We're ready for them. So, you hang tough. I will see you soon, okay?"

"Okay."

That night they returned Maestro to the prison in the manner he expected - chains too tight, bumping him into walls with their sarcastic excuses, and directly to the hole upon arrival. When they took him through the prison, the joint cheered him and he got the same welcome in the hole before the Bulls began to bang other prisoner's cell doors, yelling "Quiet! If you know what's good for ya." Maestro would not take food from the Bulls when they brought the chow around, knowing they would at the least spit in it, or worse poison him. After missing the second meal, Maestro heard a bang on the wall, and then the voice from the cell beside him saying, "Hey, man, I don't blame you for not taking that slop from the Pigs. But we are not going to see you starve in here, right fellas?" You could hear the guys yelling, "That's right!" and banging on their doors again.

The Bulls came in again and said, "If we have to come in here one more time somebody's going to be sorry!" Then slammed the door on the way out. The voice next door said, "Hey, man, share my chow. There is a space at the bottom of your door. See it?" Maestro looked down at the space, the width of the door and about two and one half inches high. "I see it," he said. "Here it comes." A second later, a bologna sandwich, wrapped in toilet paper, slid over.

"Thanks man. What's your name?"

"I'm surprised. Don't you recognize my voice? We're old friends, and enemies as it were."

To Maestro's surprise, it was Big-House. Now he wasn't sure this meal was any better than the ones from the Bulls.

Big-House said, "I know you're wondering man, don't. I was tanked that day. I know you're stand up. I just want to let you know - no hard feelings. Besides anyone who gives these Pigs what they got coming is alright with me, man."

Then the guy on the other side of him started to send stuff over, and across from him, too.

One guy down a little ways said, "Hey Maestro, you need any smokes? I got plenty."

"No, thanks."

"Well, if you change your mind just holler, my name's Hank. I'm your man." And it went on like this for the next month. Maestro was somewhat at ease. He began to meditate, stretch, and do light workouts to regain his strength, clear his mind, and prepare his spirit for what was ahead of him.

The guards began to take notice of his training routine and sought to discourage it. They would open his food slot and tell him someone was there to speak to him and then gas him in the face. They would open the slot in the middle of the night and spray him with a water hose, and then put a fan in front of the open slot for hours. They would catch rats and put them in sacks, and then open the sack so its mouth would face under the door of Maestro's cell. They would shut off his water for days at a time, so that he couldn't drink or flush. Through it all, Maestro never gave them the satisfaction of a scream or complaint. For him, once he had returned his mind and spirit back to his Special Forces training, this was child's play. The attorney got wind of their treatment of him and went to court for a restraining order for it to discontinue, with a threat of a lawsuit to follow. Then she came and visited Maestro. When she saw him she "GE'd" off on him, ranting and raving, "Why didn't you tell me? Why would you keep this madness from me?"

Maestro said very calmly, "It's not your problem. You got your hands filled with my case. Have you seen my children? Are they okay?"

She looked at him with sheer astonishment and said, "It's not my problem?"

He looked at her with cold eyes and said, "No. You haven't answered my questions."

She exhaled deeply, "They're fine. They miss you. What am I going to do with you?"

"Defend me in court."

"And who will defend you in here?"

"I will."

At her wits end, she said, "Okay. Okay. Have it your way. I'll see you soon. Trial starts next week."

She got in the car in the parking lot and turned back to give the prison another look and realized that she had just left a piece of herself inside. She had begun to care about him, something she had never felt to this extent before with a client. But then, she never had a client like him before.

In spite of the court order, the Screws kept up their torturous practices until the day before the trial. That night they came five deep, in full riot gear, opened his door and said, "You're being moved to the infirmary. Tomorrow you will meet the judge and your maker."

In the infirmary, at least Maestro would get a hot shower and good night's sleep on some dry and semi-clean sheets. When he was given his bed assignment, to his surprise, Jr. was in the bunk right next to him. He had a fractured ankle. Maestro said, "Hey, man how'd you get that flat?"

"Playing basketball. I came down on it the wrong way. The guys miss ya man. But we're trying to keep the music alive."

"What you hear about Keys?"

"Only that he's in a bad way. But he don't have long to go. If he can hang in there another two months, he'll be out, free."

Maestro took a shower, groomed himself and got in bed. Jr. said, "Say, man, it's none of my business but your daughter is bugging out because she hasn't heard from you. That's not like you. She thinks you blame her, according to her cousin Greg. But I know that ain't it."

Maestro flipped, "What you mean they haven't heard from me? I've been writing to them both."

"Well, man, those punks must be messing with your mail or something."

Maestro knew that was to be expected. "Jr., do me a favor."

"Sure, anything."

"Get word to Greg. Tell him to let her know I've been writing and I don't blame her for anything."

"You got it man. I'll take care of it in the morning, when I go for my exercise walk."

"Thanks man. I appreciate it!"

"Don't mention it Bro... You just be alright. So how's it looking?"

"Too early to tell, man." Maestro was enraged at what he heard and didn't feel like being sociable, but didn't want to hurt Jr.'s feelings. So he just told him another truth. "Look, Bro. I haven't been getting much sleep in the hole, and I have a full day ahead of me. So, I'm going to turn in, okay?"

"Sure man. I understand. I'll see you in the A.M. and breakfast will be on me."

Maestro said, "You got it man, thanks for understanding." Then he turned over and went to sleep.

## CHAPTER TWENTY-NINE

Maestro rose with the sun and just laid awake until the rest of the ward came to life. He took a shower, and passed on breakfast, as had become his practice in the hole. Shortly after breakfast, five Screws showed up in full body armor to take him to court. They put him in a van with waist chains and leg irons. One officer in front, two in the back, and two in a chase car to make sure that he did not get out. Upon arrival at the courthouse, they put him in a cell, still chained. Moments later, Shanon arrived at his cell and found him with his back turned towards the bars. She clapped once and rubbed her hands together and said, "You ready to go get'em?"

Maestro spun around quickly, glaring through rage-filled eyes that made Shanon step back, even though there were bars between them.

She said, "What's wrong?"

Maestro sternly said, "Why did you lie to me?"

Shanon said nervously, "What are you talking about?"

"My daughter…How could you keep something like that from me?

Shanon replied, "I thought it was best, I didn't want you distracted."

The light left his eyes, and ice appeared in its place. That struck terror in the depths of Shanon's soul, even though she fought hard not to show it.

Then Maestro took a step forward and said in a low voice, "You don't get to decide that. You had no right!"

Then he took a step back, and turned his back on her. Shanon said, in a trembling voice, "I'm sorry."

He said nothing at all.

Then she said in a small almost child-like voice, "I'll see you in the courtroom."

Then she left. She walked towards the courtroom, very slowly, crushed by what had just happened. She had lost his confidence and that was something she never wanted to do. She would never forget that look in his eyes, and the worst of it was, he was right. She did have no right.

When she arrived in the courtroom, her investigator noticed right away that she was visibly shaken and asked, "What's wrong?

She said, "I blew it, and I blew it bad."

"What, the case?"

"No, with him."

"Do you think that you're a little too close to this thing?"

She looked at him as if to say, "Don't overstep your bounds," but instead said, "It's more complicated than that."

"Is there anything I can do?"

Wanting to return to her good graces, Shanon, said; "Yeah, make sure I have everything I need to win this case. I at least owe him that."

"You got it, boss."

The D.A. had also witnessed that Shanon was shaken, and said to his assistant, "I think we got her on the ropes. Have the defendant brought in."

His assistant went to the phone to call the courthouse cell block, while the spectators were let in. Among them were Poo and her mother, and sister, Ebony. A whole host of off duty Screws, and the wives of the fallen, were present as well. There were even a half dozen or so reporters and news people of some kind.

Maestro was brought in still in waist chains and leg irons, and when he reached the attorney's table, Poo came running through the little gate separating the courtroom from the spectators section. A Bailiff attempted to step in her path and Maestro stepped in his. Instinctively, the Bailiff put his hand on his pistol; Maestro's eye's still angry and cold, glanced down at his hand very quickly. Then locking onto his eyes said, "If you pull it, you'll have to use it."

The Bailiff nervously glanced over at Shanon, then back to Maestro, when Shanon spoke, "It's his daughter, let them have a minute."

The Bailiff, looking for a way out but needing to save face was relieved to hear her speak, and said; "Well I'll let it go this time."

Maestro knelt down and Poo gave him a big hug that he couldn't return because of his chains, but was able to kiss her. She said, "Daddy, I made you something," and pulled a small bow from her pocket that was nicely braided. He knew that she had help with it, and glanced up at her mother approvingly and then back to Poo and said, "Why don't you hold onto it for me, so I know it will always be safe."

"Okay, Daddy."

"Thank you, baby. Give me a kiss." She did.

"Ebony, give me a hug darling." Ebony was eager to oblige.

Ebony said, "I love you, Daddy."

And Poo said, "And me, too, Daddy."

Maestro said, "I love you both. You take good care of each other, hear?"

They took each other's hand and said, "We will."

Their mother put a hand on each one of their shoulders to let them know that they had to come back behind the gate. Maestro looked up at their mother and said, "Have you spoken with Pam?"

"Yes, she won't come. She says that she cannot face you. She has not even been by the house. She called crying that night, saying she was sorry she almost got Poo shot, and you killed, and it's all her fault. She shouldn't blame herself. I told her it's not her fault and her mother told her the same thing. But she's not ready to hear anyone yet, and it doesn't help that she hasn't heard anything from you."

Maestro glanced at his lawyer with one of those looks, and then at the kids' mother, and said, "Thanks for trying."

The Bailiff said, "Okay, folks, the Judge is about to come out, so you will have to step back."

The kids' mother said, "Okay, just a second," then told Maestro, who now stood up, "I'm here today because the kids needed to see for themselves that you were not dead. But you know, because of my job, I can't be here every day."

He said, "Don't sweat it. I appreciate all you've done so far." Then he gave her a kiss on the cheek, and told the kids "Love you guys. Be good."

"We will, Daddy."

They stepped away just as the Bailiff said, "ALL RISE!" The Judge entered the courtroom and took the bench. He struck the gavel and the Bailiff said, "All be seated." The D.A. stood up to speak when the Judge raised his hand to halt him. Then he spoke:

"I want those chains removed from the defendant before we go any further. I will not have a jury see him like that." The D.A. began to protest and the Judge cut him off and said, "That's my ruling on the matter, Bailiff." The Bailiff obeyed and the chains and shackles were removed.

Judge: "Are there any motions or special circumstances we need to deal with?"

Shanon stood: "Your Honor, it doesn't have to be settled this moment but, the discovery is not complete. I just want to be on record with respect to that."

"The court orders that full disclosure be made within forty-eight hours. Doable, Mr. Prosecutor?"

"Yes, Your Honor."

"Anything else?"

"Not at this time."

"Do the people stand ready for trial?"

"Yes, Your Honor the people stand ready."

"Does the defendant stand ready?"

"The defendant stands ready."

"Bring in the jury."

The jury entered and was seated. Then the clerk stood. The Judge instructed the defendant to rise. He did. Shanon rose with him.

The clerk said, "Lloyd Day, you are before this court charged with four counts of murder, how do you plead?" Maestro declared, "Not guilty."

"You may be seated"

# CHAPTER THIRTY

"Mr. Prosecutor."

The D.A. stood and walked towards the jury saying, "Good morning, Ladies and Gentlemen of the jury. I am the District Attorney for this county and represent the people in this case. We intend to prove that this man (and he pointed at Maestro) wantonly and willingly murdered, four Correctional Officers in the performance of their duty. At the end of this trial, we will ask you to find him guilty on all counts. Thank you.

"Miss Harris."

"Good morning, Ladies and Gentlemen. I am the Defense Attorney in this case. The judge will instruct you, in order to convict, you must find him guilty beyond a reasonable doubt. I mention this fact to you because I predict through the course of this trial my opponent will speak to you as though he was on the scene and witnessed these killings.

"I submit to you that, that's what the evidence will show, that this was a killing not a murder. He wasn't there. The only person in this courtroom right now that was there is my client.

"No one is denying that people are dead, but your job after hearing all the evidence is to examine how and why that came to be. I believe when you do, you will find my client not guilty. Thank you."

The court then said, "Mr. Prosecutor, call your first witness."

"The State calls Mr. Laws."

"Mr. Laws, do you swear to tell the truth, the whole truth and nothing but the truth, so help you God?"

Mr. Laws: "I do."

"Please state your name and occupation for the record."

Mr. Laws: "Theodore Laws, former Warden at the Triple "O" Prison."

Q: "Mr. Laws, how long were you employed at the prison?"

A: "Thirteen years."

Q: "Did you know the fallen officers?"

A: "Yes, all of them very well. I made it a point to know all of my officers."

Q: "How would you rate their performance on the job?"

A: "They were outstanding officers. All of them were very professional and fair. They all would have had bright futures if that animal hadn't. ...."

"Objection!"

"Sustained. Mr. Laws you will only answer the question asked, and no more, is that clear?"

"Yes, Your Honor."

"You may proceed."

Q: "During your watch did you know the defendant?"

A: "Yeah, I knew him."

Q:"What kind of prisoner was he?"

A: "He was one of the worst kinds."

"Objection!"

"I'll allow it; you'll get a chance to cross, proceed."

Q: "What do you mean worst kind?"

A: "He was always into something. He was a manipulator, and had a propensity for violence. He led a riot last year."

"Objection, no foundation."

"Sustained, the jury will ignore that last statement. I won't warn you again, Mr. Laws."

"Sorry, Your Honor."

Q: "Were you ever frightened of him?"

A: "All the time."

"Thank you, no further questions. Your witness."

Shanon slowly rose from her chair, approached the witness stand, glanced at the jury, and then while still facing the jury, asked her first question.

Q: "Mr. Laws, why are you no longer Warden at the Triple "O" Prison?"

The Prosecutor jumped out of his seat: "Objection, not relevant, Your Honor."

"Mr. Laws just engaged in character assassination of my client and defense is entitled to examine his."

The court responded by saying, "I'll allow it, answer the question."

A: "I was dismissed."

Q: "Why?"

A: "For political reasons."

Q: "Isn't it true you were fired because you screwed up?"

A: "No."

Q: "Are you aware that the governor held a press conference right after he fired you?"

A: "Ahhh…Yes."

Q: "And you say that's not so?"

A: "Yes."

Q: "Did the Governor lie to the people?

A: "No."

Q: "Then what?"

A: "He was mistaken."

"I see, let us now move on."

Q: "You said that you knew all your officers?"

A: "Yes."

Q: "And they were "excellent," I believe is the word you used?"

A: "Yes."

Q: "And also fair?"

A: "Yes."

Q: "Then you are aware that three of them had been suspended, one of them more than once?"

A: "I have no knowledge of that."

Shanon placed a piece of paper on the D.A.'s table and had one still in her hand. "Your Honor, may I approach the witness?"

"You may," responded the court.

Q: "Mr. Laws, would you identify for the court what kind of document that is, that you're holding?"

A: "A suspension form."

Q: "And who is it for?"

A: "It was for one of the dead."

Q: "And this one?"

A: "Another of the dead."

Q: "And this one?"

A: "A third."

Q: "Now would you tell us whose signature is reflected as the person that did the suspending?"

A: "It looks like mine."

Q: "Looks like yours? Is it or is it not your signature?"

A: "Yes."

Shanon in a coy voice said, "Okay, then."

Q: "Is this your idea of excellent men?"

"Objection."

"I'll withdraw the question."

Q: "You also said that you knew my client?"

A: "That's correct."

Q: "How many times have you had my client put in the hole?"

A: "I don't remember."

Q: "No one goes to the hole or at least stays there past an hour without a signed order from you, is that correct?"

A: "That's procedure, correct."

Q: "How many times did you sign one on him?"

A: "I don't remember."

Q: "Your records show none. Does that surprise you?"

A: "Well, we gave him a lot of breaks."

Q: "Is that procedure, too, Mr. Laws?"

"Objection!"

"Sustained."

Q: "Mr. Laws, isn't it true that this man has never been in the hole?"

A: "He must have."

Q: "I thought you don't remember?"

A: "I don't."

Q: "But, this is a man that you know?"

A: "Yes."

Q: "Like you know your officers, right?"

"Objection!"

"Withdrawn."

Q: "Who trained your officers?"

A: "Lt. Rambone is the training officer."

Q: "Have you ever heard the term B.W.I.B.?"

A: "No."

Q: "You're sure?"

A: "Yes."

"No further questions."

The court said, "Call your next witness, Prosecutor."

"The State calls, Warden Bristol."

Warden called and sworn.

Q: "Warden, would you describe the events of these brutal murders?"

"Objection!"

"Sustained."

Prosecutor states, "I'll rephrase."

Q: "The events of the day of the tragedy."

A: "There were three officers assigned to the Visitor's Center. One of them noticed that one of the visitors had something in their mouth and he had reason to believe it was drugs. So the officer attempted to retrieve it. That's when Mr. Day there entered the visiting room and went berserk, murdering all three officers present."

"Objection!"

"Sustained. The jury will disregard the last statement."

Q: "What happened next?"

A: "One of the officers had pushed his emergency button on his radio, signaling our special squad, which is the only squad allowed firearms within the compound. They arrived and the defendant there

190

tried to take them on, killing one of them. The other two got off one shot apiece and brought the defendant down. He was taken to a local hospital where he had surgery and remained in their care until approximately six weeks ago. He was then returned to us and placed in a secure unit to await his trial."

"Your witness, counselor."

Q: "By secure unit, you mean the hole, don't you?"

A: "That's what some call it."

Q: "This visitor that was suspected of having drugs in her mouth, was a five year old child, was it not?"

A: "I suppose so."

Q: "Just how exactly did this officer attempt to retrieve what he allegedly perceived to be drugs?"

A: "My understanding is he asked her to spit it out. She attempted to swallow it, and he proceeded to apply the Heimlich maneuver in an attempt to bring it up, for her safety of course."

A bunch of guards burst into laughter at this point and the Judge banged his gavel.

Q: "Are you attempting to make light of this incident, Warden?"

A: "No."

Q: "Who taught this officer the Heimlich maneuver? Freddy Kruger?"

"Objection!"

"Withdrawn."

Q: "Isn't it true that when my client entered the Visitor's Center, your officer was choking his daughter to death?"

A: "That's not the way I heard it."

Q: "Where did you hear it?"

A: "From the Special Squad officer on the scene."

Q: "Did he witness the incident?

A: "He must have, he made the report."

Q: "Aren't there laws that protect the attacking of children?"

"Objection."

"Rephrase."

Q: "The handling of children by your officers?

A: "In Triple "O" Prison, I am the law!"

Q: "I see, and who appointed you, God?"

A: "The Governor."

The courtroom erupted in laughter again, and the gavel sounded again.

Maestro just glared.

Q: "You take pleasure in what you do?"

A: "I take pride in what I do. You have to keep these people in line or they'll run amuck."

Q: "Who are 'These people?'?"

A: "Don't start that crap with me. I treat them all the same, black, white, purple. He's a killer, plain and simple. You have to watch his kind. They will smuggle, kill, you name it, and their families, too."

She just let him ramble and put his foot in his mouth, she knew she would bury him and the other Warden later, but, first she had to lay the tracks.

Q: "What is the defendant's prison record?"

A: "I can't say. I only came aboard six months before this happened, and many of the records were destroyed in the riot that preceded me."

Q: "They destroyed them? So, in effect, you don't know what he's like?"

A: "I know his kind."

Q: "I see, what you describe as "his kind" can't be trusted; will do anything. Are any of that kind on your staff?"

A: "Of course not."

Q: "Have you ever heard the term, B.W.I.B.?"

A: "No."

Q: "You're sure?"

A: "Yes."

"No more questions at this time, but, Your Honor, the defense would reserve the right to recall this witness back and the previous one."

"So noted. Call your next witness."

The State called the State Coroner, who was sworn, and described how the officers died.

"Call your next witness."

The State called Sgt. Weeks. Weeks called and sworn.

Q: "Sgt. Weeks, can you tell us just what you do?"

A: "I am attached to the special unit of the Triple "O" Prison."

Q: "What does that mean?"

A: "It means whenever there's a problem that moves beyond the control of the patrolling officer, then we are brought in to deal with it."

Q: "Were you among those brought in on this day?"

A: "I was."

Q: "Please describe to the court and jury what you observed and did?"

A: "The alarm was sounded and that indicated that there was a serious situation in the Visiting Center. Myself and officers Malice and Sift responded. Upon our arrival we found three officers down and the defendant in a crouching position with some chicks."

"Objection!"

A: "I mean some females. We ordered him to stand up and he did. Then he charged us, killing Frankie. Then he began to cry, the performance of a lifetime. Then, I and Officer Swift each fired our weapons because we were in fear of our lives."

"Thank you, no further questions. Your witness."

Q: "You were in fear of your life when you fired? Is that correct?"

A: "Yes."

Q: "Do you know where you hit him?"

A: "I learned later that it was in the back. But, he was moving so fast. He was spinning like a top."

Q: "Have you lied about any of your testimony?"

A: "No."

Q: "You sure you don't want to change any of your testimony?"

The Screw glanced over at the D.A. and back to Shanon and said, "No."

Q: "Have you ever heard the term B.W.I.B.?"

A: "No."

Q: "You're sure?"

A: "Yes."

"No more questions at this time."

State called Mrs. White. Mrs. White sworn and seated.

Q: "Mrs. White, could you tell the court where you were on Father's Day?"

A: "I was at the prison visiting my husband."

Q: "Can you tell us what you saw?"

A: "I saw those guards just doing their jobs. One of them walked over to that little girl and told her to spit out what she had in her mouth. Then the bigger girl jumped on them, saying "leave her alone," and he shoved her. And the little one kicked him in the shin."

Poo screamed "Uh-uhhhh!" The gavel fell and Maestro turned to Poo and put his finger up on his lips, indicating to her to be quiet. Poo said, "But Daddy, it's not so." Maestro said, "I know" and winked at her. Poo calmed down and the questions continued.

Q: "What happened next?"

A: "Then he came in (let the record show she means the defendant) and he went berserk. They tried to stop him, but he knew that karate stuff, and he killed those poor people. Then three more came in with guns and a bunch more without guns. They told us to get out of the way. He tried that karate stuff on them, too. But he only got one. Then they finally got him."

"Thank you, no more questions. Your witness."

Q: "Mrs. White, what is your husband in prison for? Tell us, Mrs. White!"

"Objection! Irrelevant, Your Honor."

Shanon, "May we approach, Your Honor?"

"Approach."

"Your Honor, the defense contends this witness is lying; being motivated to do so, her credibility is questionable. Submit she's trying to make life easier for her husband with her testimony, and we have the right to pursue it."

D.A., "Your Honor, her husband's record has absolutely no relevance in these proceedings."

"I'm going to allow some leeway, counsel. Go slowly."

"You may answer the question."

A: "He's in for rape, but he didn't do it."

Q: "How many of those rapes didn't he do?'"

"Objection!"

Court, "Rephrase."

Q: "How many counts of rape is he in for?"

The witness looked at the D.A., then the Judge, who instructed her to answer the question. Then in a very low voice, the woman on the stand said, "Eight."

Q: "Could you speak a little louder please?"

A: "EIGHT!"

Q: "Did anyone make you any promises for your testimony?"

She looked at the D.A. again, nervously, and said, "No."

Q: "Are you sure you want to leave your testimony as it is?"

Again she looked at the D.A., then said, "Yes, I'm sure."

"Okay, no more questions." Then the D.A. rose and announced, "Your Honor the State rests"

"Okay, this court will be in recess until nine a.m. in the morning." The jury was dismissed, and the Judge asked to see both counsel in chambers.

Maestro was shackled and returned to the prison hospital ward for the night. The conference with the Judge was to make sure full disclosure to the defense would be made by the end of the business day to determine what, if anything, would be needed.

"Defense requests a T.V. and VCR."

That evening, she went up to the prison to speak with Maestro, who hadn't spoken since the expression of rage shown in his courthouse cell, with the exception of his comments to his children and their mother.

When she arrived at the prison, Shanon learned that he had been removed from the infirmary and taken back to the hole. She protested to the Warden, whose response was, "We're not in the courtroom, now counselor. We're in my backyard."

"He's well enough to travel. He's well enough to return to the hole. You're his lawyer, so I can't stop you from seeing him, but he stays in the hole. You still wish to see him?"

"Yes."

He told his Deputy to arrange it. Maestro appeared in the small room with the table and two chairs just for that purpose. He noticed right away that Shanon was upset. She was mumbling something about who do these people think they are. Maestro hearing her statement responded, "Asked and answered in court today, wasn't it?"

She looked at him and said, "Well, let's see what the answer is tomorrow. Are you alright?"

"Now what could be wrong with me? I'm back in the hole, and I don't know what shape my child is in."

"I know the timing is bad, but I need to ask you for your permission to put the kids on the stand."

Maestro shouted, "Out of the question!"

Shanon said, "But they..." (before she could finish, Maestro said);

"No buts. The answer is 'no.'"

"Okay, I just needed to know. I just wanted you to know how sorry I am about not being honest with you about your daughter."

"While we're being honest, if you want out, you're off the hook."

"Why would I want out?" Shanon said.

"I was in the courtroom today, sober. It didn't seem to go all that well for me."

Shanon sneered at Maestro, which surprised him and got his attention. "I told you when I arrived I was no slouch. Today was their day; tomorrow's ours, unless you want another attorney."

"Nope, not my style. I'll be in the courtroom tomorrow and I plan to take the stand, whether you're there or not is up to you. I've given you your out if you want it, and won't hold it against you."

Shanon got up abruptly and looked, at him almost in the same way he had her, and just said, "Good night," and left.

That night, when Shanon got back to the office, the investigator was waiting for her with evidence that would blow the prosecutor's case out of the water. All she had to concern herself with now was how she was going to present it.

Maestro returned to the hole, Hank from down the hall hollered, "Hey, Maestro, how's it look man?"

"It looks like they're about to catch hell."

"Why you say that?"

"They pissed her off and I helped."

"Ha!"

The guys thought Maestro had lost his mind, but Maestro just smiled inside. The next morning, the procedure was the same, with the goons that took Maestro to court. When he entered, Shanon and the investigator were already there. Shanon said, "Good morning." Maestro just nodded. Shanon said, "This is Bill Masters. He works for me. You have him to thank for many of the weapons you'll see used today." Maestro shook his head without saying a word and then took his seat. It was time: all rise, be seated, formalities out of the way, bring in the jury, they were seated.

The Judge said, "Ms. Harris."

She rose and said, "Thank you, Your Honor. She looked down at Maestro with that "Hold on, here we go now," look. He looked at her and said in a low voice, "Go get'em partner."

She smiled and said, "The defense calls Officer Bruce McMan." He was called and sworn, and Maestro said, "Well, I'll be damn!  It's the mailman."

"Good morning, Mr. McMan."

"Good morning."

Q: "You are an officer at the Triple "O" Prison, are you not?"

A: "I am."

Q: "How long have you been there?"

A: "23 years."

202

Q: "In that time, you must have seen quite a bit."

A: "I would say so, yes."

The D.A. looked on with an eyebrow raised.

Q: "Have you had the occasion to know my client?"

A: "Sure, he spends his out-of-cell time at work on the outer crew and what is called the Music Box. He runs a band in the prison and they play for the prisoners, and sometimes for the families. In his cell, he's always writing his kid or meditating."

A:"How do you know that, writing his kid, I mean?"

A: "I'm the Mail Officer, I always take his mail. He stands out because he never gets mail back, but that doesn't stop him from writing anyway. He was real big on being a father to his kids. We even had one or two conversations about it."

Q: "Does the name Thomas Wayne mean anything to you?"

A: "Yes, he was another prisoner. They were in the same band. They call him Keys. I think he plays one of those piano, organ things, poor kid."

Q: "Why do you say that?"

A: "Because of what happened to his mother and all."

"Objection! Relevance, Your Honor."

"A little latitude, Your Honor?"

"Overruled, please continue, Mr. McMan."

A: "Well, they found the woman dead on the side of the prison road after she was turned away."

Q: "Does the term B.W.I.B. mean anything to you?"

A: "Yes."

Q: "What does it mean?"

A: "It means the Brotherhood Within the Brotherhood."

Q: "Could you tell us about it?"

A: "Well, it's a group of white officers. . ."

"Objection!"

"Overruled!"

Q: "Are you one of them?"

A: "Not as a member. But I used to be a supporter, you know, of the ideals."

Q: "Which were?"

A: "Pro white, you know."

Q: "You don't support them anymore?"

A: "No."

Q: "Does it have to do with my client and the prisoner you describe as Keys?"

A: "Yes."

Q: "What?"

A: "Well, I was among those that were trapped in the riot last year. The riot began over this Keys guy, and after it did, your client there took control of it, the riot I mean. When it was over, those two were targeted by the B.W.I.B. for vengeance and frankly, even though I wanted no part of it, I was prepared to look the other way."

Q: "Well, what brought you here today?"

A: "Their method of vengeance!"

Q: "What do you mean?"

A: "They went after their families; first that poor woman, that kid Key's mother, come all the way from God knows where with that child and they turned her away just to be cruel. That poor woman was elderly, and they even refused her a drink of water in all that heat."

Q: "You witnessed this personally?"

A: "Yes, I was out front sorting the mail; she dropped dead on the road trying to make it home. When they realized what had happened, they put her son in the hole before they told him, concerned that he would be hard to manage. When he became distraught they shipped him off to the State Hospital to cover themselves, and if that wasn't enough, they went after this guy's kids. They gave her that candy out front, and then tried to say they suspected drugs; they set up that child. I have children of my own, and like I said, I know he was crazy about his. I can't be silent about something like that."

"I know this testimony will make you unpopular with your peers. I appreciate your courage and your honesty. No further questions. Your witness."

Q: "Mr. McMan, as you said, you were captive in the riot. Weren't you threatened with death at one point?"

A: "Yes."

Q: "How did you escape that fate?"

A: "He stopped it."

Q: "He, the defendant?"

A: "Yes. He saved me and the officers' lives, by stopping those who wanted to kill us. He even got into a fight with the most dangerous prisoner we have."

Q: "But he's the most dangerous prisoner you have, isn't he?"

A: "Not in my opinion."

Q: "You were grateful for your life, weren't you?"

A: "Of course."

Q: "Isn't this whole testimony just pay back? I mean, you have your time in, full pension anyway, so you're lying to pay him back, aren't you? Aren't you?"

"Objection! Badgering, Your Honor."

"Withdrawn!"

The D.A. announces, "I'm done with this, this person."

"Call your next witness."

Defense calls. . . Several visitors were called to describe what they saw in the Visiting Center that Father's Day. All described the same thing:

"That man was killing that child, her sister tried to help and the officer knocked her down and she hit her head. Their father walked in, and when he saw what was going on, he went to help his children. Instead of the other officers helping the poor child, the officer tried to stop the father from helping his child. And that's why the man lost it."

Call your next witness.

Defense calls, Lt. Rambone.

Lt. Rambone sworn and seated.

Q: "Lt. you train the officers, do you not?"

A: "Yes, that's correct."

Q: "What is their objective?"

A: "Their objective is to keep their brother and sister officers safe, and maintain control over the prison at all times."

Q: "So, if there's a disturbance between an officer and a prisoner, does the responding officer ever ask, for example, what's going on here or whose fault is it?"

The courtroom erupted again in laughter, the Lt. asked Shanon, "Girly, are you on something?"

Shanon replied, "I assure you that I am in full control of my faculties."

The Lt. stated, "They don't ask any questions, they secure the area where the problem is as quickly and forcibly as possible. There is no fooling around with these people."

Q: "Are they never right?"

A: "They are the criminals, lady. We are the good guys."

Q: "So, it is safe to assume that when a prisoner is involved in a confrontation with an officer, and other officers arrive on the scene, that they will be against him?"

A: "It's better than assuming that they're there to be his home boys."

More laughter, and the sound of the Judge's gavel. . .

"No further questions. Oh, just one more:"

Q: "Have you ever heard the term, B.W.I.B.?"

A: "...No."

Q: "You're sure?"

A: "...Yes."

"Thank you, that's all."

"Your Honor, the defense moves to show a video tape."

"Objection! Relevance, Your Honor."

Shanon continued:

"Your Honor, the Visiting Center is outfitted with a video camera to scan the area for contraband introduction to the institution. This is the tape of the Father's Day incident."

The District Attorney flipped out: "Your Honor, how do we know it's authentic?"

Shanon replied, "We had it authenticated, Your Honor, by the prison's own expert. It was in discovery."

The Judge allowed it.

The video was shown to the jury. Afterwards the D.A. requested a recess and offered a deal for reduced charges, if Maestro pled Guilty. Shanon's laughter was heard throughout the courtroom.

Recess over.

Defense calls Lloyd Day.

Maestro took the stand and was sworn.

"Let's get right to it," Shanon confidently said while using the center of the courtroom as her stage.

Q: Would you explain to the court and jury the events of last Father's Day?"

A: "My children had planned to visit for six weeks. They wanted it to be a Daddy and Daughter's Day. The three of us were excited about it at that period of time. I was called for the visit and when I arrived, I heard a commotion of some kind but could not see because others were blocking the view. When the path was clear, I saw that my oldest daughter was on the floor injured, possibly dead, and my youngest being killed by this grown man. I started towards them and my path was blocked by an officer, who appeared to be reaching for his weapon. There was also one coming up behind me doing the same thing. I struck them both and proceeded to my daughter. The one that was killing her looked over his shoulder and saw me coming, and just slung her like a rag doll and tried to run; by which time I was taken by rage. He stopped and turned to make his stand, and it was over before it really began. I then went to examine my children when I heard someone say, 'Freeze.' I turned around and was ordered to stand and move away from them, which I did. Then my youngest, apparently afraid, seeing that they were going to kill me, ran towards me. When she did, one of the men turned his gun on her and I stopped him. It's all on the video you have just seen. "

Shanon answers Maestro by saying, "Yes, I know. I wanted to get a fix on your frame of mind at that moment."

Q: "And now do you have any remorse about your actions?"

A: "I am always troubled by the loss of a life by my hands. Having said that, I don't have any apologies to make for going to the aid of my children."

Q: "But you are a prisoner and there are rules?"

A: "I am a father first, and I never intend to honor any rule that would forbid me from aiding my children."

Q: "How's your wounds?"

A: "Healing."

"Thank you, no further questions."

Your witness.

The D.A. approaches the stand and looking at Maestro, asks his first question:

211

Q: "Mr. Day, what sent you to prison in the first place?"

A: "Manslaughter. Two men attacked me in a parking lot."

Q: "And now, this is your answer to dealing with all your problems?"

A: "No."

Q: "But you are quite a violent man, are you not?"

A: Yes, beyond a certain point, and under the right circumstances, I suppose we all are."

D.A., "We are not talking about anyone but you!"

A: "Perhaps that's the problem."

Q: "Oh, you have a handle on the problem, do you? Suppose you share it with these good people."

A: "Well, since you asked... A gun, an instrument of death, is licensed in line with the constitution for the purpose of defending life and/or property. Those like yourself would have that apply selectively, in that only some people enjoy such a right or take such a position. Well, as I have said, I am a father first. I need no one's permission to protect my children and you would seek no one's either, so why don't we get rid of the hypocrisy, first. If I had died in that Visiting Center that day, or my children, these good people would never be assembled to sit in judgment on guards. There would

212

have been an announced investigation into the matter, and then they would have been invited to take bows of heroism.

"So, who's kidding who here? My children have committed no crimes and done no wrong. They are supposed to be treated with the respect and dignity that you expect yours to be. It simply is not alright with me, and would never be alright, that grown men trained in warfare can visit upon my children terrorism of any kind."

"That will be enough, Mr. Day."

"Well, you asked."

The whole courtroom was stunned and clearly pondering what they had just heard. The D.A. was clearly sorry that he had stepped in that. He expected to see Maestro flip out and hang himself. Now his job was to try and paint him as a monster.

"Very nice speech."

Q: "You were trained in the military were you not?"

A: "Yes."

Q: "You had training the average soldier doesn't get, isn't that correct?"

A: "Yes."

Q: "With that training comes control and discipline, doesn't it?"

A: "I suppose."

Q: "Why didn't you just shove the officer aside, or knock them down? Huh, why?"

The D.A. said in a voice that indicated, now I got you.

Maestro cleared his throat and said in a very calm voice,

A: "When I saw the condition of my children, I knew I had to get to them quickly. Those that would prevent me from doing so, I only wanted to contend with once, not over and over along the way. So, when I struck out, it was with the intention of applying enough force for them not to recover in time to detain me further. I knew what their next move would be, as a matter of their training, and that was to kill. Indeed that's what they attempted to do. I was not of the mind that I was in a contest. I was of the mind that I was at war, and they were at war with me."

The D.A. said, "And like you do in a war, you just killed, and killed and killed! I'm finished with him." (In an attempt to cut his losses and have the last word.)

Witness may step down.

Your Honor, the defense rests.

Prosecutor you may start your summation.

"Thank you, Your Honor. Ladies and Gentlemen of the Jury, you have heard a lot during the course of this trial, I'm going to attempt to sort it out for you. While it is sad and unfortunate that a grandmother died and two young children were hurt, this is not a trial about them. This is a trial about a cold blooded and brutal murder of four officers at the prison, who also have grandmothers and children. That man right there! That menace to society! That admitted killer! Willfully took the lives of four prison guards. He could have knocked them unconscious, but he chose to kill them. You have heard sworn testimony of other officers that this is a dangerous man, and I ask you to say to him today, that he will never get a chance to be dangerous in the world again, by finding him guilty on all counts. Thank you."

Ms. Harris.

"Thank you, Your Honor. Ladies and Gentleman, the Prosecutor has just called my client a killer four times, and you know something? I don't take issue with that. (Surprise was shown by all as she went on.) Unfortunately, four prison guards were killed, but I submit to you they were not murdered. I further submit to you that my client is the manifestation of two positions that all good parents have ever held. How many parents have said, "I will move heaven and hell for my children?" And how many have said, "God help those who would hurt my children"? This man moved hell away from his children. Most parents would go berserk if you slapped their child. This was far more than just a slap. Just imagine walking into a room and seeing your 17 year old sprawled out on the floor, and the feet of your 5 year old dangling in the air because some out of control man, is choking the life out of her. What would your reaction be; to think about some set of rules or man-made laws? I think not! I think you would have, as he did, obeyed natural laws. You must ask yourself if you found your children under attack, would it matter what the attacker did for a living?

"My opponent wants to make a big deal out of my client's training. Consider this: he's been in that prison for seven years and there is no evidence that he has ever raised a hand in anger except to save the life of his child. You've seen the tape. It was there. You have heard from the honest witnesses, they were there, and you heard from my client, he was there. You have also heard from two Wardens, the Lieutenant, and my opponent. They were not there! Yes, this case was about some killings, but the charges are murder. My client did not leave his cell that day and say, "I think I'll go down and murder some people." He went down to enjoy a special day with his children and found them under attack in a most vicious way, and went to their aid. Ladies and Gentleman, he is guilty only of being a protective father and loving his children to death. Pardon the pun. He was right when he was on the stand, and I think you know it. You good people would have never been called to convene on the officers if they had killed him, they would have called it a justifiable homicide even though they had the guns. But the prosecution will argue that theirs are the only killings that can be justified or understood. I submit to you that my client Mr. Lloyd Day finds in the lives of his children as much importance as the prison officials find in the lives of their officers. Should we blame him for that? I think not, and I believe you know that, too. I'm asking you to have the courage to say so. Thank you."

The jurors were then instructed in the law and sent out to deliberate...

All rise. As they stood, Maestro said to Shanon, "Nice job." She said, "Thanks, that's high praise coming from you."

The Bailiffs came and put the cuffs on Maestro. Then he turned to Shanon and said, "No matter what happens from here on, I'm satisfied that you did your best." Their eyes locked and she was moved by the sentiment and relived that his eyes were softer now, and filled with sincerity. He turned and they took him away. She could do nothing but stand there, and even though she felt she had done her best, she still felt helpless, feeling the need to somehow do more.

The jury make up was about as balanced as one could ask for, without being unreasonable. There were six men and six women. There were four Blacks four Whites, two Spanish, one Asian and one Indian. Every major faith was represented, and even one or two that were not considered major. The range of their stations in life peeked at middle class and descended to just above getting by. Their collective professional experiences, for the most part, put them in touch with common people on a day to day basis.

Of the female jurors, there was a secretary, a guidance counselor, a psychologist, a kindergarten teacher, a housewife, and a perfume salesperson.

Of the men there was a construction worker, a truck driver, an owner of a car wash, a high school coach, a factory worker, and a toll booth operator. The owner of the car wash was clearly the older of the members.

They had all been attentive to the evidence presented during the course of the trial, and gave full attention to closing arguments given by the District Attorney, as well as the defense attorney. They seemed to give the same attentiveness to the instruction in the law given by the judge.

They were now ready for the task given them, and intended to embrace it with the seriousness that should be given to the fate of any human being. The alternate jurors were placed on stand-by, in the event another could not complete his or her charge.

The clerk called the roll, and the jurors were lead out.

## CHAPTER THIRTY-ONE

The jurors were assembled in the jury room.

"Okay, I guess the first order of business is that we elect a foreman. Anyone got any ideas? Yeah, how about Mr. Wilten? He is the oldest, no offense,"

"None taken."

"I subscribe to the theory that with years comes wisdom, and some whipper-snappers, no offense,"

"N-O-N-E taken." Ms. Shawmut said with a raised eyebrow.

"Okay, then that's settled, unless anyone objects. "No one did. "Well, should we begin with a vote, or a discussion?"

"I vote for a discussion," one juror stated.

"Anyone object?" was asked by the foreman. No one did.

One juror began the discussion with, "Well, he is already in prison, and for killing, mind you. So he's no angel, let's begin there."

Another juror weighed in with, "I guess you got your mind made up!" Where upon there was an eruption of conversation, pro and con.

The exchange went on between eleven jurors, the foreman being one of the eleven, sympathy was expressed repeatedly for the families of the fallen guards, and much was discussed about crime in America in this day and time. Tempers flared around racial issues and a couple of jurors let their horns show from time to time. Breaks were taken for meals and entertainment, because they were sequestered, and then a return to the same.

Yet, no one had called for a vote. Three days into this battle of intellect and vision, with most of them near their wits end, a young woman of the jury turned to the only one who had gone unnoticed in the midst of all the hoopla -the one who had not spoken, the gym teacher, and said, "What is your take on all this? You have said nothing." Soft-spoken and reflective he began, "Well, first let me give you a sense of who I am and perhaps that will help you better understand how I arrived where I am. I am a college graduate and I coach high school sports. During the course of my work I meet a lot of young people and a lot of parents and have come to know the ways of both pretty well. I am also a parent of three; my youngest is seven, like the defendant's. I should tell you that my observation is that it matters little to him what we do in here. He has long ago made his peace with it."

"What do you mean?" asked the foreman.

The coach went on and had everyone's undivided attention. "When the prosecutor spoke of him, I saw a prisoner, yes, even an animal. When his attorney spoke of him I saw a defendant and some resemblance of a person. And then, he himself took the stand and I saw and heard a father and a man. I don't know how many of you are parents, but for those of you who are, I know you have said or felt, 'May God have mercy on those that would harm my children because I won't', and you have said and felt this with little or no regard to personal consequences. The difference between us and him is we have not faced the test he has, but I expect, God forbid, if we ever had to, we would vote to come out of it the way he did. We hope that we would have the courage to step up and answer the cry of our young without hesitation and after, I suspect, we would feel just within ourselves, grateful to God for victory, and whole in the eyes of our young. We were called upon to judge the facts in this case and were instructed by the Judge, in addition to the law, not to leave our common sense at the door."

"I would like to think as a man and a father, that there is no fury on this earth or beyond that I would not face for my children. And as a man and a father, I can think of nothing that would move me to take a child off her feet by the neck. For me, the choice, while not easy, is simple. I must judge him the way I would judge myself, and I submit, when you come to your vote you must, as a matter of justice, do the same.

Three days, five hours, twenty-three minutes later, there was a verdict. Everyone was notified and assembled in the courtroom.

The Judge entered the courtroom. "All rise. Be seated. Bring in the jury." The jury was brought in and seated. The Judge said, "Ladies and Gentlemen, have you reached a verdict?"

"We have, Your Honor."

"Please give the verdict slip to the Bailiff."

They did, and he delivered it to the Judge, who read it without expression, and said, "You have agreed on this verdict one and all?"

"Yes, Your Honor."

He returned the verdict slip back to the Bailiff who returned it to the jury foreman. Then he said, "Would the defendant rise?"

Maestro stood, and Shanon stood beside him. The Judge said, "Ladies and Gentleman, what say you?"

The jury foreman held up the slip and said, "While we find that the defendant did kill, we find that he did not murder, and therefore find the defendant 'Not Guilty' on all four counts."

Maestro leaned forward, palms down on the table, almost in a collapse, and shook his head forward as if to say, "Yeah, alright." Then he mouthed the words, "Thank you," to the jury. Shanon was all over him giving him a big hug and he hugged her back, saying, "Take a bow, Lady. You did well."

Meanwhile, the voice of one of the wives screamed, "What!" Then the courtroom erupted, and the Judge banged his gavel repeatedly calling for order. More Bailiffs began to enter the courtroom, and people mumbled and cried. When the courtroom had returned to order, the Judge thanked and dismissed the jury. Then he said, "Mr. Day, the jury having found you not guilty on all indictments, you are dismissed. The Court further orders that you be released from the hole and returned to the general population of the prison and no further steps to be taken to punish you for this matter. So ordered."

This Court stands adjourned.

The media was in a frenzy. Shanon went out front to take them on.

## CHAPTER THIRTY-TWO

There was a knock on the door at the home of Pam, whose mother opened it to find Shanon, the attorney, standing there. "Hello," she said, "I hope I'm not intruding. Would you mind terribly, if I had a moment with Pam?" Pam's mother responded, "Not at all. Please come in." As she did so, Pam emerged from her bedroom, obviously hearing the request.

Shanon spoke, "Hello, Pam." Pam simply raised her hand and said, "Hi." Shanon said, "Do you mind if we talk?" Pam shrugged her shoulders, and said, "Okay." Pam's mother gestured them both to the living-room and asked Shanon if she could get her anything. Shanon graciously declined and she and Pam proceeded to the living-room.

As they sat, Shanon asked Pam, "Did you hear the news?" To which Pam replied, "Yes, it's all over the T.V." Shanon told Pam, "I'm sure he would love to have you and Poo by his side, at this time of triumph." Pam said, "I'm still not ready to face him." Shanon rose from her seat, and went and sat beside Pam on the couch. She took her hand and said, "You know why I became a lawyer? When I was a young girl, not much older than your sister, I used to love to tag along with my father. It was still a time when racial relations were a far tilt to one side. My father was a carpenter, and a good one. He put the steeple on the local church all by himself. He was a man that stood six foot five inches, and that was enormous for those times. One day he had to go to the hardware store for supplies for a job he had to do, and I wanted, as always, to go to town with him. This day he said, "No, it would be too dangerous because of all the trappings in the store, which I could get into and hurt by." (Neither of us knew at that time, how right he would turn out to be). Anyway, I fussed and screamed and he gave in, as he often did, and took me along. When we got to town, we stopped first at the ice cream shop, where he bought me this big ice cream cone, and said, "Don't tell ya mother." He made me sit outside of the hardware store on a bench that doubled as a bus stop, and he went inside to pick up what he needed. Like the child I was, I could not keep still, so I got up and walked just a couple of feet away to a gift shop that was next to the hardware store. I became fascinated by the things I saw in the window and lost track of my bearings a bit. Just then a man, a white man as large as my father, walked out of the gift shop. I will never forget he wore a beige suit and a white straw hat and some brown tie up shoes. I did not see him until I turned and bumped into him. The cone tipped and the ice cream landed on his shoes. He had a gift under his arm and the sight of my ice cream hitting his shoes, startled him so that he dropped the gift. That angered him and he yelled, "You little nigger bitch," and slapped me, just as I looked up at him to apologize. I also, in that same moment, saw my father as he walked out of the store just in time to see the man strike me. The light in my father's eyes went out and this look of rage came over the face of this gentle giant, and he killed that man on the spot with his bare hands. When they came to arrest him they took me to the station too, where they would call my mother to pick me up. I asked to be with my daddy and the policeman told me only three kinds of people are allowed back there: criminals, policemen, and lawyers. It was at that moment that I decided that somehow I would be a lawyer, so I could get back there. I never saw my father free again. He died in prison and for years before his death, I blamed myself for him being there, until I was your age.

"My seventeenth birthday, my mother took me to see him for the last time. She knew he was dying, and so did we. Through tears, I kept saying how sorry I was for what happened. If only I had listened to him and not moved. At seventeen, I was still his baby, he took me and sat me on his lap and said 'look at me.' I did. He said 'do you love me?' I said, 'yes, Daddy." He wiped my tears with his large fingers and said 'never ever cry about this thing again. It was not your fault. You followed the laws of nature being curious. You understand?' I told him, 'Yes, Daddy.'

I followed the laws of nature, when I acted as I did, because my children's enemies are my enemies. That man died by his own hand and you must never, never take the blame for that, you hear me? Yes, Daddy. Do you understand me? Yes, Daddy. Do you believe me? Yes, Daddy. Good, now give Daddy a big hug and a big kiss. That made it alright for me, and it made it alright for him.

"I took your father's case because it reminded me so much of that time in my life. I was not able to help my father, but I'm so happy I was able to help yours. But it's not finished."

"What do you mean?" said Pam.

"When he learned that I had kept those matters about you from him, I saw the light go out in his eyes replaced by the rage I saw in my father's for that man. I need to make that right with him and that's why I'm here. Your father, as was mine, is a very proud man, his children's enemies are his enemies, and he would have none of his children them take the blame for the actions of their enemies. He would want you to know that. Here's my card, my home number is on the back. I hope you will think about what I've said here today. I will be going to see him tomorrow to tie up some loose ends; I hope you will go with me. If you don't, I will understand....

"I believe I was drawn to this case because our fathers are kindred spirits, which makes us kindred sisters." She stroked her hair and smiled, "That's the way I hope it will always be. Think about what I said," and she rose to leave.

Pam's mother stood in the doorway, moved by what she had just heard, and gave Shanon a nod of approval. No words needed to be spoken between them; she just showed her out, hugged her daughter, and left it at that.

# CHAPTER THIRTY-THREE

Maestro was taken out the back, and hustled back to the prison. Upon his arrival he was greeted by the Warden who was flanked by two of his goons.

The Warden cut off his path, glared and said, "The only reason you're still alive is because of those videos of the records that you got out of here."

Maestro quickly scanned the goons before locking stares with the Warden. He never spoke, but his body language was loud. It said, "Is that so? We may have to see about that." Then he moved past the Warden a few steps before breaking the stare, causing the Warden to make a half turn to maintain it. He scanned the two goons again and then he was gone inside.

He was sent back to his old block, as ordered by the court. The word had reached the prison before he did, and the guys were all but out of control.

They cheered and gave him high fives and pats on the back, saying things like "Good going." He looked for and found his partner Shot, and they did the dance of reunion. He saw Greg, who told him that he received and passed on the message. Maestro went to the phone to call Pam, but got no answer. Then he went down to the Music Box where he was sure to find the rest of the gang, and he did. They all cheered and said, "Let's make some music man."

Just then they heard a voice behind them saying, "Anybody looking for a key board player?" They looked up and it was Keys. "Well, I'll be dipped and haunted for seeing a ghost! How did you get here?"

"After McMan testified at your trial, they took me off those drugs, detoxed me and here I am, at least for a minute. I go home in a week, so let's cut an L.P. before I go." They all laughed and said, "Sure, dude!" Then Keys stepped to Maestro and said, "I'll never forget all that you've done for me, man. If there's anything I can do for you..." Maestro said, "As a matter of fact there are a few things." Keys quickly said, "Name it."

"Find your son and take care of him. Start a band and save me a spot." And then in a whisper, "Sue their ass off, for your Mom." Keys smiled and said, "You got that, Bro..."

Maestro said, "Well, let's get started on the L.P." They chuckled and got to jamming.

About two hours into it, a Screw came and got Maestro, telling him he had visitors. Maestro went and cleaned up, then went to the Visiting Center.

He saw Poo, Ebony and their mother. Upon entering the Visiting Center he caught a flash back of the last time he was there, but that quickly vanished when Poo and Ebony came running to meet him yelling, "Daddy!"

People in the Visiting Center began to point and whisper. Maestro swept them both off their feet and into his arms with huge hugs and kisses and carried them back to where their mother was seated. She rose to meet him and gave him a hug also, saying, "Congratulations! You're all over the news. Your lawyer is real proud!" Then she added, "I think she has a thing for you."

Maestro said, "Thanks for coming. The kids look great and so do you." She smiled as if to say, "I know you're just being polite."

Maestro sat with Poo on his lap, and Ebony and their mother flanking him. She said, "I'm sorry things got spoiled between us, and I never want to add to your heartache but, I can't come here. I'll be lucky if I can make it a couple times a year. I will try to make sure you see Poo on her birthday, and maybe like Christmas, but that's about the best I can do. And I'm sorry about the way things worked out between us, too, because I never want to lie to you again."

Maestro replied, "I understand and appreciate what you've done, and whatever you can do. I'm sorry about the way things worked out, too." Now Maestro went on to say, "I think you know that you will always be important to me, and I hope I to you."

Poo interrupted and said, "Well, who's gonna bring me, Daddy? I want to see you." Maestro stroked her braids, but before he could answer, there was a voice, a familiar voice that said, "I'll bring you!" They all turned and looked up in surprise, and looked into the eyes of Pam standing there. Pam looked down at her father and said, "Can we talk?"

Maestro extended his hand, palm up, with eyes filled with love and said, "Always!"

Pam took his hand, and Poo's mother stood to give up her seat, and stood behind the chair. Pam sat in tears saying, "I'm sorry and..." Maestro cut her off saying, "Oh No. No. There's nothing to be sorry about. Now stop these tears." Pam wiped her eyes and turned to Poo saying, "Hey Kidd-o," and then to Ebony, "Hi, Ebony."

Maestro said, "How'd you get here?"

Pam raised her eyebrow, causing Maestro to look behind him, finding Shanon standing there. Pam went on to say, "We had a good talk. She explained things to me. Please don't be mad at anyone."

Maestro, with the head of Poo and Pam resting on his chest, reached back with extended hands, one for Shanon and one for Leitha. Ebony got up and stood behind Maestro with her hands on his shoulders, and while Maestro's attention was on giving looks of appreciation to Shanon and Leitha, Ebony was being mischievous and gave the signal to Poo and Pam, that his neck was exposed and vulnerable for tickling. They went for it and their Father started laughing a fit, while the kids' Mothers and Shanon joined in the mischief by holding on tight to his hands so he could not defend against the attack of affection.

During it all, Poo would think through the memories of music, filled with songs of love, celebration and freedom.

The war was over, but the battles would rage on. My family was whole again and even extended, and the healing had begun for us all around.

The wives of the fallen guards would raise their voices beside those of the guards' union in protest of the verdict, and times would get harder for prisoners in the name of blue brotherhood.

Yet, the next song my father would sing would be of undying gratitude. "What a world, huh?"

J. Jabir Pope is a man of integrity and compassion. He crafts stories to enlighten and inform. To learn more about Mr. Pope, visit his Amazon.com Author Page, as well as www.favoritesonsproductionscom. Or, if you are the writing type, reach out to him at:

Joseph Jabir Pope

2 Clark Street

P.O. Box 43

Norfolk, MA. 02056

42907552R00130

Made in the USA
Middletown, DE
25 April 2017